NIGHT OF THE WALKERS

G.W. Mullins

LIGHT OF THE MOON PUBLISHING

ISBN: 978-1-958221-23-5

First Printing

This is a work of fiction. Names, characters, businesses, places, events and incidents are either the products of the author's imagination or used in a fictitious manner. Any resemblance to actual persons, living or dead, or actual events is purely coincidental.

Light Of The Moon Publishing has allowed this work to remain exactly as the author intended, verbatim, without editorial input.

Printed in the United States of America

For further information, on his writing, visit G.W. Mullins' web site at http://gwmullins.wix.com/books

For books available from G.W. Mullins in Hardback, Paperback and eBook

Visit: https://gwmullins.wixsite.com/books

Or scan the QR Code below

Links to G.W. Mullins pages are on Linktree
https://linktr.ee/gw.mullins

What begins as a simple, bittersweet tale about a man turned into a polar bear, grandly unfolds into a rich, mythical adventure, in this best-selling book series.

Based on Hans Christian Andersen's fairy tale, author G.W. Mullins expands on this classic story creating a new mythology that takes readers into the land of snow and ice.

G.W. Mullins

Rise Of The Snow Queen
Book Series

The Polar Bear King
War Of The Witches
The Story of Gerda and Kai

Rise Of The Snow Queen Series

What begins as a simple, bittersweet tale about a man turned into a polar bear, grandly unfolds into a rich, mythical adventure in this best-selling book series.

Based on Hans Christian Andersen's fairy tale, author G.W. Mullins expands on this story creating a new mythology that takes readers into the world of snow and ice.

Long before the adventures of Gerda and Kai, this story takes readers to a remote mountain village, where winter claims lives, at the Snow Queen's command. The story goes back to the Mirror and how it cracked, sending its shards into the world to infect the innocent.

This reimagining, embarks on a much more adult tone with the mood turning rather sinister, as the Snow Queen battles to obtain the mirror. The story will capture and pull you in as Gerda and Kai make their appearances by the third book in the series.

Rise Of The Snow Queen Series

Book One: The Polar Bear King

Book Two: The War Of The Witches

Book Three: The Story Of Gerda And Kai

From
The
Dead
Of
Night
Book Series

Death is only the beginning.
Daniel walked in the land of the Dead.
Now the Dead want him back

Daniel Is Waiting

Daniel Returns

Daniel Awakens

Daniel's Fate

G.W.
Mullins

From the Dead Of Night Series

Death Is Only The Beginning. Daniel walked in the land of the dead. Now the dead want him back!

Daniel Stratton died in a tragic accident. His life should have been over, but it was not. His spirit spent the next sixty years trying to communicate with the people who came to the cemetery. Then, Jen came one night to the mausoleum, seeking refuge from a life that was spinning out of control. It was there she found Daniel.

As they work to free him from the cemetery; they learn that the Light comes for all dead, Daniel is forced to enter it. Inside he sees seven Shadow People within the light, and each one marks him. Daniel knows these Shadows will come for him. Each one in the body of human who has just died. To survive, Daniel and Jen must escape the "Shadows" that are coming for them.

From the Dead Of Night Series

Book One: Daniel Is Waiting

Book Two: Daniel Returns

Book Three Daniel Awakens

Book Four: Daniel's Fate

Best-Selling Author G.W. Mullins speaks to the
dead and talks about
After Death Communication in his book series...
Messages
From The
Other Side
Stories of the Dead, Their Communication, and Unfinished Business
Messages
From The
Other Side
G.W.
Mullins
Messages
From The
Other Side
G.W.
Mullins
Messages From The Other Side

Crossing
Over
Mullins
Crossing
Over
Mullins
Crossing
Over
Mullins
Crossing Over

Available in Hardback, Paperback and eBook

Messages From The Other Side Series

Best-selling author G.W. Mullins shares his personal journey towards understanding death, the afterlife and communication with spirits of loved ones who have passed over. In "Messages From The Other Side Stories of the Dead, Their Communication, and Unfinished Business," Mullins tells of dealing with the grief of his mother passing and the reassurance of an after death communication that totally changed his outlook towards death and grief.

This book not only tells of Mullins' personal journey into understanding but also guides others to understand why we receive communications and the signs to look for. Mullins also explores visitation dreams and tells of his own personal experience in the area and shares the stories of others who have had similar experiences.

This book highlights the author's personal journey in an exploration for knowledge, and his understanding, without question, there is life after death.

Messages From The Other Side Series

Book One: Meassages From The Other Side

Book Two: Crossing Over

In order to save his uncle, Malachi is forced to summon
Santa Muerte, the deity of death. With his soul on the
line, he must do her bidding, to regain his freedom.
To fight evil, you have to
embrace the darkness
Rise
Of The
DarkLighter
From Best-Selling Author
G.W.
Mullins
Dark Awakening
Night Of The Demon
Available in Hardback, Paperback and eBook

Rise Of The Dark Lighter Series

Mullins returns to the familiar world he created for the "From The Dead Of Night" series, while building a new story in this universe. In the book "Daniel's Fate," Mullins left his audience with an ending that promised more. In this latest book, he delivers with a continuation of the final battle between good and evil.

In order to save his uncle, Malachi is forced to summon Santa Muerte, the deity of death. He offers a year of his life in exchange for her help. With his soul on the line, he must do her bidding, to regain his freedom.

The dead begin to rise, as Angels and Demons prepare to wage war for control of humanity. Malachi must choose a side as Armageddon begins.

"Dark Awakening" is the first of three books from "Rise Of The Dark Lighter." This new series is a continuation of his "From The Dead Of Night" books.

Rise Of The DarkLighter

Book One: Dark Awakening

Book Two: Night Of The Demon

Vengeance
A Paranormal Murder Mystery

"Mystery, Murder, Paranormal Events, and a story that leaves you guessing as the bodies stack up."
– Matthew Trent OutLoud Magazine

After the death of her father, Danni starts a new life in a seaside town in New York where she and her mother move into a strange Gothic house with a terrible history. From the moment Danni gets there, she feels she is being watched. She is sure they are not alone in the house.

As Danni learns of her new home, she is told of a past resident who fell to her death on the nearby cliffs at the same time that her teenaged daughter, Elizabeth, disappeared.

Elizabeth's spirit, appears to Danni and claims that her mother's death was a murder, not suicide and asks for Danni's help in bringing the dangerous killer to justice.

The mystery unfolds as Danni enlists the help of the hunky new friend she has made named Joe. A romance develops between them, but does Joe know more about the murder and disappearance than he is letting on? Will Danni live to solve the murder?

Dream Walker Series

They say a dream is a wish, but what they forgot to mention, nightmares are dreams too. As the city darkens and humans descend into sleep, a powerful being enters the Earth Realm. This mysterious creature, known as the Sandman, takes control of our dreams and battles for control of souls.

After a boy named Zach is taken into the other realm, he awakens to a new world filled with nightmares. He is joined by two others, Daniel and Jen, as they battle to escape the Dream World, and find their way back to reality. Beware the Sandman is coming.

"Enter The Sandman" is the first of three books from Author G.W. Mullins' "Dream Walker" book series. This new series, shares a couple of familiar faces from the Best-Selling "From The Dead Of Night" books, featuring the Best-Selling titles "Daniel Is Waiting" and "Daniel Returns."

Dream Walker Series

Book One: Enter The SandMan

Book Two: Wide Awake In Dreamland

Nick Grainger

Book One

The Curse Of Cleopatra

G.W. Mullins

Nick Grainger Series

Building on the concept that the Earth was once populated by a superior Ancient Alien race, this new book series takes the reader on an adventure through gateways to the multiverse.

Nick Grainger, a young college student working on an archaeological dig in Egypt, accidentally activates a gate to a different universe. He along with three of his companions, are thrown into the ancient alien gateway system between parallel worlds. Lost in the multiverse, they must search for a way home.

On their journey, their gate opens into strange new worlds, similar to their Earth, but in different times and in places. It is on one such Earth, they arrive in Egypt, not as it was in the days of the ancients. Now, it is a place where a technologically advanced race of gods rule.

These new gods of Egypt live through taking the bodies of human hosts. It is there, Nick must fight his ultimate battle, as he is designated to be host to the god Anubis.

"Nick Grainger The Curse Of Cleopatra" is the first of three books from Author G.W. Mullins' "Nick Grainger" book series.

FROM THE AUTHOR OF "RISE OF THE SNOW QUEEN - THE POLAR BEAR KING" AND "DANIEL IS WAITING"
THE LEGEND OF WHITE BEAR
Extended Edition
EVERYONE HAS A BEAST WITHIN THEM.
G.W. MULLINS

The Legend Of White Bear (Extended Edition)

Nita's tribe faced the coming of the bear every full moon. When it came, many would die.

To protect his daughter, the chief sent her away to live in a rip in time and space, called the void. He told her it was for her protection, but he never told her of the bear history.

One member of his tribe, was burdened with carrying the bear shapeshifter trait. For a lifetime, they would be cursed with being both human and bear until their death. Then a new child would be born to carry the trait.

While in the void, Nita discovers the true horrifying history of the white bear.

THE CONVERGENCE
BOOK ZERO
MASS DESTRUCTION
WELCOME TO THE BEGINNING OF THE END
From the Author of the Best-Selling Book Series
"Dream Walker." Inspired by the artwork of C.L. Hause.
G.W.
Mullins

The Convergence Series

In the year 2029, the third world war will begin. After the global population is pushed to the brink of insanity from the recent pandemic, they plunge into hatred and violence. With the space race to colonize the moon, man seeks a refuge from the insanity, and the impending environmental destruction brought on by decades of pollution.

In the worldwide confusion, the inevitable happens, when a single nuclear warhead is fired by the command of an insane dictator. Nuclear retaliations are sent forward, ending in a destruction of the Earth's moon. The end of mankind as we know will begin. Human civilization is cast in ruin. A strange new world rises from the old; a world of mutation, super science, and magic. Witness the Convergence. The countdown begins now.

The Convergence Series

Book Zero: Mass Destruction

Book One: Armageddon

Other titles available from G.W. Mullins include:

Timeless - An Adult Paranormal Romance Novel

Aliens, Gods, And Other Paranormal Native
American Tales

The Native American Story Book Volume 1-5-
Stories Of The American Indians For Children

Walking With Spirits Volumes 1-6 Native American
Myths, Legends, And Folklore

The Native American Cookbook

Star People, Sky Gods And Other Tales of The
Native American Indians

More Star People, Sky Gods and Other Paranormal
Tales Of The Native American Indians

23

For Clarence

Life is wasted on the living.
*~ **Anonymous***

In their paper "When Zombies Attack: Mathematical Modeling of an Outbreak of Zombie Infection," a University of Ottawa research team concluded that a large-scale zombie outbreak would lead to societal collapse unless dealt with quickly and aggressively. The New York Times *included the work among its top ideas of 2009.*

*~ **Matt Mogk***

Before ☣ The Beginning If The End

"Jason, come look at this." Stephanie called out.

"If you are trying to get me to look at some star or flicker of light, I am not interested." Jason called back sarcastically.

"No, I don't mean anything like that. There is something out there, in space. Just not something that should be there." Stephanie began to get frustrated with him. "look, if I didn't think it was important, I wouldn't bother you."

"I knew the minute you got this telescope; I was in for it. Now, show me what you think is so important."

"You know, when you became my boyfriend, I thought you would at least take some interest in my hobbies."

"Well, I thought when you became my girlfriend, you would spend a little more time on earth with me, instead of out there in space." Jason snapped at her, as he threw his hand up and pointed to the stars.

"Would you just look?" She insisted.

"OK, what am I looking at?"

"The telescope is already pointed at the right location. Just look through the lens." Stephanie spoke, as she guided his body into place.

Jason looked through the eye piece, and squinted his eyes, until the image came into focus. As he stared, he exhaled. Then he started to speak, but fumbled his words. He pulled away for a moment and then returned to the telescope. He couldn't believe his eyes.

"That… looks like…. a ship or something. It's not from the earth. That's not possible. How can that be there?" He asked her.

"I don't know…I don't know what it is, or who could have brought it here. The one thing I do know, is it's big. We have never had anything like that size on earth before."

"Maybe it did not come from the earth." Jason tried to contain his excitement.

"Wow, I guess my obsession with space isn't so boring now, huh?"

"I get your point. I am sorry to treat you like that. Now, what do we do about this?" He asked.

"We can report it, and see if the government takes it seriously. I mean, we are two 16-year-olds who saw a spaceship. That's not crazy, right?"

"If we can see it, they can too." Jason insisted, as he turned back to the telescope and looked through. "Steph, there is something odd about this ship."

"Yeah, what?"

"As it is spinning, you can see through it. Like there are holes that go all the way through."

Stephanie reached for his shoulder, as she moved him out of the way. As she leaned in, she pulled her long blond hair back, and over her shoulder. As she leaned in, she studied the ship as it drifted lifelessly through space. She magnified the image as much as she was able to. Then she saw it clearly.

"There is a lot of damage. That ship has been in battle. There are several open holes in the outer hull. We have to contact someone. If that thing doesn't continue to float, it could lose orbit. I wouldn't want to know the damage it could cause, if it crashed down in a city."

"What do we do, just call NASA, and say we have visitors?" Jason said, trying to be funny.

"I wouldn't say it like that, but I would give them a location to investigate, and a reason."

Stephanie broke down her gear, and packed up her bags, as they began their hike down from the high mountain point. She ran the whole scenario through her head, over and over again, as they walked. She was excited about the possibilities of what was happening. She was also frightened of the secrets the ship might hold.

"Why are you so quiet?" Jason said, trying to get through to her.

"Just scared." She replied.

"Why? It isn't like it's the end of the world. What could be the worst thing that could happen? The ship, is filled with aliens, who come down and kill us all?" He laughed.

"I'm not sure there is anything left alive up there. So, no I am not so scared of that. It's just, that ship, means we are not alone in the universe. Who knows what these people are like…or were like."

"Steph, you saw just what I did. That ship could not hold life. There are holes in it. If there was anything on it, it is dead. They may have been the last of their people. The thing we do know is, someone kicked their butts."

"Yeah, and that someone, could do the same to us." She sighed, thinking about it.

"Maybe, but maybe not. Let's just turn this over to the guys who handle these things. Unless there is a government coverup, they will let us know the facts."

"Here's hoping, because I just got a cell signal. I am searching for the number and calling."

Jason turned away, as she dialed the number. He stood there looking up to the spot where the ship drifted. Despite the dark coloring on the outer hull, Jason could swear, he could see it without a telescope. A feeling of fear ran through him as he shivered. Maybe he thought, Stephanie was right to be afraid.

Chapter One ☣ A Month Later

"It's amazing, isn't it?" Colonel Anderson said, looking at the zoomed image, on the screen in the front of the room.

"Yeah, it is. As long as it does not crash down into a major city, or populated area." Jeremy Donavon answered him.

"The first contact we have with a possible alien craft in years, and you just go negative." Anderson said, turning away from him.

"Look, I am all for finding life out there. God knows, we get enough reports of 'little grey men' every week. And we all know; this is not the first craft to come near the earth. I am just saying, we need to be careful."

"That is a given, especially since its orbit is decaying. I checked the telemetry this morning." Anderson said, with a grim look on his face. "If it continues on the track it is taking, it will collide with the International Space Station."

"Is anyone besides the USA doing anything?"

"No, they are acting as if they don't see a thing out there. The Russians have been tracking it, but they are in such a screwed-up state, with their ongoing wars. No one else, has anything in development, that can get out there fast enough to do anything. So, I guess…it is up to us to save the day." Anderson said, as he turned back to the screen, and watched the derelict ship.

"Wonderful! Well, we were going to unveil the new NASA shuttle series anyway. Guess this is as good a time as any. Colonel, how many people are currently on the space station?" Donavon asked.

"Seven…and of them, four are Americans. Doesn't really matter, we are not going to let anyone die on our watch. The shuttle, and crew have been preparing for the last two weeks. They should be ready in time."

Donavon made a noise, that sounded half like a laugh. The colonel turned to look at him. He was confused by the sound. He made a face and waited for a response. "Something funny Donavon?"

"Not so much in this situation, but we have all heard rumors of the dark satellite, that so many have claimed to have seen. This ship is really dark in color, almost black. Could this be what people saw, or is it related to the satellite of legend?"

"The Black Knight is just a myth. Everyone says it is just space junk. If it was really out there, we would have dealt with it by now. I wouldn't lose any sleep because of it." Anderson turned to leave the room, as Donavon staired at the dark foreboding ship.

<div align="center">~~~~~</div>

Above, in geostationary orbit of the Earth, the hulking ship continued its journey, drifting forward. As its path continued towards the space station, it hit several satellites along the way. Many were just decommissioned trash, left to float until they burned up on reentry.

As the ship began to pass by the moon, a signal began to generate, as if it was triggered by its presence. The signal bounced all through the outer reaches of space, until it found its target. From the darkness of space, a satellite began to move. It drifted slowly at first, then ignited jets to propel it towards the ship.

As the light of the sun bounced off its slick black exterior, the Black Knight came to life. It matched the speed of the war beaten craft, and came along side. When in range, it scanned the surface and collected data from the long since dead ship.

When it was done, the Black Knight processed its data and turned toward the moon. It sent an initial beacon, then waited for a response. The satellite, did as it was intended. It was created to observe life on and around the earth.

It had been there since the beginning of man. It had been silent, except for situations it had to report back about. In its memory, were the great events on earth from the changing of continents, to Pompei, World Wars 1 and 2, the launching of nuclear weapons and nuclear power plant melt-downs. It stood by, silently recording it all.

Its last files were of environmental destruction. It was filming the countdown to possible end of life. The giant black satellite, hung in the sky performing its task, always waiting to send the data to its relay station.

In the many centuries that had passed, it was successful at its task, but these later signals did not seem to be received…until now. The satellite, broadcast its data flow towards earth's moon. At first there was silence, then a response. On the dark side of the moon, deep within a converted cavern, a light lit up. Then screens lit, and the space illuminated.

The cavern came to life, as computers came online. Not like the computers we know; these were beyond anything man ever imagined. These electronic systems, were alive and intelligent.

As the signal sounded, a robotic drone was sent to the surface. It traveled quickly through the dirt and debris to its hidden destination. As it stopped, it broadcast a return signal, to transmit all stored data.

As the drone entered a structure, hidden to anyone looking at the surface, it rolled through the hall looking to either side, at the pods that stood upright. All glowing, all preserving life, after the thousands of years they had been entombed there.

As the robot made its way to the end of the hall, it approached the electronic controls. It sent out a light beam to the computerized system. The message was short and to the point…Awaken.

Chapter Two ☣ The Truth Is Out There

Jason looked up to the sky in wonder. He hadn't taken space seriously before. That was then, now since seeing the ship floating in orbit, things had changed. Stephanie joined him on the rooftop as they looked out, trying to locate the ship again.

"Is it entirely safe for us to be here?" Stephanie spoke, with a nervous quiver in her voice.

"It's just a roof top. You will be fine, just stay away from the edge." Jason said smiling, knowing he was rattling her nerves.

"It has been a month and still, nothing is happening. What are they waiting for?" Stephanie moaned.

"It is typical government crap. They cannot do anything without votes and fighting. Personally, if it were me making the decision, someone would have been there trying to figure out if this ship came for a reason. They might have been a part of a ship sent to annihilate us. Just saying." Jason scanned the sky as he ranted.

"I don't know, it they wanted to kill us, they could have already. This ship has been ripped apart. They already tried to take someone on. Why come here? Unless, we just happened to be conveniently in the way of their drift."

"Steph, we will probably never know. You know how the past alien visitations were covered up. There have been too many leaked events. This will be, just another supposed weather balloon, or something."

Stephanie looked at him and smirked. "Jason, how could they cover up something, you could see so easily? If we saw it, then others did too. Besides, that thing is drifting, which means it does not have power. No power, no maintained orbit. It will eventually crash. Try covering that up. In the age of everyone having a camera in their cell phone. There is no hiding that truth."

"Yeah, I guess you are right, but what happens when it crashes? How many will die?" Jason's face changed; he was not so lighthearted. His mood shifted to a darker place.

~~~~~

The shuttle was in its final tests, as it was prepared for launch. The crew knew it was a rushed mission, still they did everything they could to ensure the ship got off the ground safely. Colonel Anderson, watched from the ground, as the booster rockets were installed and tested.

He swallowed hard at the idea they could fail. This was not his first mission. Back when he was new with NASA, he trained on an early shuttle mission. The ship was ready, everything seemed fine. Then, just after launch, the ship climbed into the air, as the boosters exploded. The shuttle was engulfed in flames, and crashed back to earth. The crew didn't survive. It was then, Anderson
~~~~~

considered giving up his life's dream of working in the space program.

He stood there staring, and for a moment lost himself in the grief. He only snapped out of it, as he heard his name called out over the speaker system. He turned to see Jeremy Donavon, waving to him from the control room windows.

As Anderson headed down the hall, he knew whatever he was being called to, was not good. He stopped short of the door and took a breath. He could feel the anticipation of bad news. He steadied his nerves, and let go of the past memories before turning the door handle.

"OK, hit me with it." Anderson belted out.

"You need to see this. Something is happening out there." Donavon said, with his face looking pale.

"What am I looking at?"

"That is the ship, we have been watching." Donovan said shakily.

"Yeah, you called me up here to see that?" The colonel snapped at him.

"No sir, I called you to see…this."

As Donavon pointed to the screen, he enlarged the area, just to the side of the ship. Anderson moved forward, and stared at the screen. He turned and looked away, and then looked back again. He could not believe his eyes.

"Is that what I think it is?" Anderson asked in disbelief.

"Yeah, I think so. I think we can remove the label of myth, from the satellite. The Black Knight is real."

"Well Donavon, I think I owe you an apology."

"No, you don't sir. I would have never totally believed it either. But there it is. It is real, and better yet, it is alive. That thing has energy readings."

"How the hell can that be. It is floating trash, just like the ship. If it has been around as long as it has been reported, how does it have power. Its cells would have depleted over time." Anderson looked on in disbelief.

"That's the thing. You are thinking in terms of our tech. This is alien, and it could replenish by terms of solar power, or whatever. Who knows how they constructed it. And get this, it is broadcasting a signal."

Anderson turned to him. "A signal, to who or where?"

"That's the funny part. It is aiming at the moon."

"There's nothing alive on the moon. We've been there." Anderson stood dumbfounded.

"Did you ever wonder why we never went back? Did we find a reason to stay away? Or were we told to?"

"The government wouldn't hide something like that…would they?"

Chapter Three ☣ The Power Of Two

"Steph, get in here. The have news about the spacecraft." Jason screamed through to the kitchen.

"Jason, I am not deaf. Although after that, I might have some damage to my ear. What's going on?" She asked.

"They have news about the shuttle launch, and now there is something floating outside the ship. It looks like a big black cylinder."

"That is no cylinder, it is a satellite. I have heard of this…the Black Knight. It has been seen so many times throughout history. Everyone said it was made up or misidentified. I can't believe it is real." Stephanie said, staring at the television screen.

"What does all this mean?" Jason mumbled, trying to make sense of it all. "Does this mean they are from the same place? Are we being invaded?"

Stephanie turned to him, and took ahold of his hand. "Calm down, it doesn't mean anything. Well, maybe, it means they are from the same creators. The ship is dead, we know that much. When you have a hull breach, whatever is onboard is either frozen to death, or it loses whatever containment to support life. Just calm down, and listen to what they have to say."

The broadcaster showed images of the satellite floating alongside the ship. They explained that full details were unknown at the time. Any information they had, was leaked and not supplied by the government. Then a closeup of the satellite showed flashing lights on its surface.

"That thing is functional." Jason blurted out.

"Not only functional, but communicating with something. Why else would it be lit up like that?"

"Steph, that thing will be there when the shuttle arrives. They said so, while you were in the kitchen."

"I wonder if they will try to bring anything back? They will have to investigate before they do anything to the ship." Stephanie smiled, as ideas flashed through her head.

"Steph, I hate it when you look like that. What are you thinking?" Jason dreaded to ask.

"What goes up, must come down. We can be there when the shuttle lands. Maybe with some high-powered binoculars, we can get a glimpse from a building nearby." She said as her eyes lit up.

"You know that is illegal, right?" He responded.

"Only if we get caught. The flight info has to be online. This is a huge event, someone had to have leaked it."

Stephanie did her research online, and in minutes, had secret government information that was hacked from a supposedly locked down system. She quickly added what she found to her phone. The shuttle was to launch the next day, with a minimal crew. If all went as planned, it would be climbing towards space by 9 A.M. Scheduled return was for two days later. Stephanie smiled, as she started a mental list, of everything she would need for the return.

"Can we talk about this? You are suggesting we break the law. And I am not talking any old law. You want to break into a government facility, and interfere with what might be one of the biggest government coverups of our lifetime. Hell, anyone's lifetime." Jason grabbed her by the shoulders, and stared into her face.

"You are right, this is big. I just feel like I have to do this. I can't just sit back, and wait to be told half of the information, when my life might be at risk."

"You are right. What if this ship crashes to earth and explodes at a nuclear level. Who knows how many people would die." Jason's expression changed. "I'd want to know if I was about to die. This isn't about what the government wants us to know. It is about protecting ours and other people's future."

"So, we do this. Not just for us, but for the other people who can't protect themselves." Stephanie kept hearing her words over and over in her head, as she reached out for Jason. She did not want to be an innocent bystander anymore.

Mullins

Chapter Four ☣ Explore And Recover

As the boosters fired, the shuttle lifted upwards, aiming towards their planned window of departure. Without any mishaps to deal with, Colonel Anderson stood on the cement slab near the launch pad. He could finally breathe. His fears were defeated one more time. He made a mental note, to work on his panic mode, before the next launch.

As the shuttle climb, the boosters fell away and the ship was under its own power. The two astronauts onboard, looked out the front windows at the disappearing sky in front of them. Turning to look at his partner, Major Tony Allen began to smile. As Captain Steven Roberts turned towards him, they both let out a laugh, and felt the release of their success.

As the ship flew across the sky, the press on the ground filmed their ascent until they were out of sight. It took hours from the time they left the atmosphere, to the arrival at the International Space Station. As they moved in closer, their shuttle disappeared in the shadow of the derelict ship.

Allen studied the craft, as it floated between them and the moon. He was amazed how small the shuttle was in comparison. He wondered how many lifeforms were originally onboard. For a moment, it scared him. This ship could have been an invasion force, if not for its destruction.

Roberts looked over at his old friend. They had been through so much together, in life and space. He was happy they had come on this mission together. There was no one he would have trusted more with his life, although he hoped it would never come to that.

"That is so much more than I ever expected." Allen said under his breath.

"I know. And it is our job to get over there, and investigate the ship, before it loses anymore of its orbit." Roberts responded.

"And how do they expect us to do that?"
Allen asked.

"Well, put simply, one of us has to go out
there in a suit and pay the neighbors a visit." Roberts
said, looking at him with a quirky smile, knowing
Allen would hate the idea.

Allen shook his head as if to say no. Roberts,
just watched his best friend go into panic mode. He
knew this would not be easy. Neither, was excited at
the idea, but it had to be done.

"Don't worry, I will do it. Besides, I need
you here to monitor the ship." Roberts smiled at him,
seeing there was fear on his face.

"I don't care who does what, I just don't want
to lose my best friend." Allen said, extending his
hand.

"I'll be careful. They said we just had to look
around over there, and bring back a couple of relics.
Then we plant a few charges, and blow that thing
onto another path."

"And if this doesn't work?" Allen asked.

"Then we get over to the space station, rescue the crew, and get the hell out of the way, as this behemoth goes down." He stopped for a moment. "Oh, and pray for anyone, or anything it it's way."

"And what about the satellite?"

Roberts looked over to the window. "I think we better stay out of its way. That thing is powered up, and we do not know what it is capable of. They said it was sending signals to the dark side of the moon."

Allen ran his hand over his eyes, and rubbed them for a moment. "Is there more to this that we should know?"

"Not that they are telling us. Makes you think something is hiding on the moon. I kinda wonder do they know what it is?" Roberts started to unbuckle his belt as he turned in his chair. "Look, if something bad goes down, and this is way bigger than we thought. Don't wait for me. Get the shuttle out of here. Save yourself."

"We'll see. You know I have never been good at following orders." Allen began to laugh, as he studied the ship directly in front of them.

Roberts put on his space suit, as he flashed on his career to that point. He was a decorated officer and his career was his life. If not, he might have married and had a family. He did not regret his choices. He was proud of his accomplishments.

"How's it going back there?" Allen's voice came through on their com link.

"Is it too late to turn around and go home?" Roberts joked.

"Yeah, I think the boys back at NASA, would be a little pissed at that idea.

"I thought so. Maybe I should just go ahead and do this."

"Just be careful. Get back here fast." Allen said, shaking his head at the whole thing.

"Have I ever let you down?"

"No, and don't make this the first time.

Roberts locked down his helmet, as the oxygen supply began to come through. Everything checked out as he approached the airlock. Then he stepped into the space, and the inner door shut behind him.

He turned to the outer door, and it opened slowly, as he floated into space. Roberts looked at the vastness around him. Floating forward, he used the jet packs on his suit, to carry him towards the ship.

As he floated past the satellite, he looked over at the activity of its lights. They flashed more quickly, as he came along side. "This thing is most definitely alive." He said, as he quickly moved himself towards the ship.

Roberts studied the holes in the hull and moved towards the largest of the lot. He looked inside as he got closer. He could see what was once a bridge, with seats and control panels. "Oh my god, this thing is so much more than I ever imagined. Allen, can you see my cameras?"

"Yes, I am reading you, both in audio and camera. Where the hell did this thing come from." Allen asked.

"I don't know, but it is impressive, and if fully functional, deadly."

As Roberts moved deeper inside the opening, he looked around for signs of the crew, but saw nothing. As he stepped down on the floor of the ship, a siren began to sound. He turned to see where it was coming from. As he moved quickly to try to make sense of it all, he never saw the lifeform floating towards his back. He was knocked to the floor, as he let out a scream.

"Roberts, are you Ok?" Allen called out to him, with no answer.

Mullins

Chapter Five ☣ Spirits Of The Dead

"Roberts what happened! Are you alright?" Allen screamed into his communicator. "Damn it Steven, answer me."

Allen waited for what seemed like an eternity, for something, anything. Onboard the derelict ship, Roberts felt the slam of his body, against the cold metal frame of the interior wall. The blow, hurt down deep inside his lungs, like someone had knocked the wind out of him. He struggled to hold onto the wall and regain his breathing.

Roberts slid down the wall and sat on the floor of the ship. Looking out, he saw the shuttle floating alongside. For a moment, he was awestruck by the ship he was in, and the size of it. He took a few deep breaths and tried to regain normal breathing.

"Allen, I read you. Just had to get my air back. I was hit from behind, by what I believe is one of their frozen crew members." Roberts spoke, as he studied the rip in the hull, and the room he had settled into.

"You scared me with that one. All I could hear was your scream."

"Allen…Tony, I am alright. I am beginning to explore the ship. Keep the coms open, I do not know how shielded this thing is. I will keep you up to date on my progress, as best I can."

"I'll be here waiting your next contact." Allen sat back in his seat, relieved his friend was safe.

Roberts moved through the remains of the ripped open room, using his jet pack to jump over the open spaces. The ship was obviously built for a much larger lifeform that anyone from earth.

As he approached the door to the interior of the ship, Roberts studied the panel to the left of it. He was not sure how to activate it. There was power still flowing through the ship. He touched his hand to the pad, but nothing happened. Then he looked to the side, and saw his frozen friend.

"I don't want to take advantage of you, but I need a little help." He said, as he grabbed hold of the body, and drug its hand over to the pad. He turned the body around, to land the palm of its hand down, and the surface lit up. "Thanks." He said, as he watched the door begin to open.

Behind him, he noticed a change in the ship. As the door opened, a protective shield formed over the rip in the hull. Roberts almost panicked, as he realized he was now locked in. When the door opened, a gush of dust and debris flowed into the room, coating him and everything in its way.

Wiping the dust from his helmet visor, he looked inside the ship. The power flowed through the passageway in front of him. He was cautious, not knowing if anything could still be alive in there. Scanning the area, he learned the ship was airtight and there was breathable air.

Moving from room to room, Roberts studied the enormous layout of the ship. He was in awe of the technology, which was so far in advance of anything on earth. Then he realized, this ship was old, very old, this tech was from the past, and yet still in advance of what humans knew. "You guys put us to shame thousands of years ago. Pity we cannot salvage this floating city."

Throughout his exploration, Roberts found the dead crew of this spaceship. It seemed no one survived what happened to them. He was not sure, but he figured they had been at war with someone or something. Unfortunately, he could not make any sense of their computer system, or how to retrieve the information. The ship would crash long before anyone could be brought onboard to investigate it.

"Allen, can you read me?" He asked, as he held tight to his communicator.

"Roberts, I can barely make you out. There is a lot of interference." Allen answered back.

"Just wanted to let you know, I am alive, and the crew is dead. No survivors. I am going to look for anything I can bring back, and then return to the ship."

"I read you. Just get back here safely. Allen out."

Roberts made his way through the never-ending hallway. Many of the rooms looked like living quarters, while others were storage. He found little of value, or that he could determine a use of. At the end of the hall, he opened a doorway to find what looked like a science lab.

He moved about the room, and saw the standing cryogenic tubes. He walked past them one by one, as he looked in, at life forms that had been stored within. They were filled with species that were unidentifiable. Some looked similar to, but not the same as humans. There were some that looked reptilian in nature. Then at the end, there was one, that looked like a female from earth.

Roberts wiped the glass-like substance that covered the window. He stared in, at what he believed to be a human woman. She was in a suspended state. He studied her, wondering if she had been abducted from earth. He wondered how this was possible. She looked as if she could just wake up and still be alive.

"I can't leave you here. If you are human and from earth, I have to bring you back with us. Maybe our scientists can revive you." He said out loud, as if she could hear him.

Roberts studied the pod she was enclosed in, and realized it was moveable. The unit had its own power source. If he could get it back to the section of ship with the battle damage, he might be able to push the pod out into space and control it, as he traveled back to the shuttle.

As he maneuvered the pod towards the door, he saw something out of the corner of his eye. As he moved, it began to pulse, flashing colors and reacting to his presence. He studied and assumed it was a power source or computer. As he turned to leave, he grabbed it in one arm as he steered the pod down the hall. He had made his assessment of the situation and was ready to leave.

Chapter Six ☣ Resurrection

"Allen, I am on my way out. I just have to make a security shield deactivate, and then I am on my way back, with some alien tech and a visitor."

"Roberts, I think you just broke up on me. Did you say visitor?"

"You won't believe it until you see her. She is amazing, and in cryogenic sleep."

"Are you sure bringing her back is safe? What if she is contaminated?" Allen became concerned.

"It will be alright, we will keep her in the load area, safely away from us. When we get home, the scientists can worry about opening her chamber. For now, I am just interested in getting out of here, and changing this things trajectory."

"I read you. Get back here as fast as you can. Allen out."

As Roberts entered the room he had first visited, he studied the layout and the computer. The onboard system, did not extend the shield until he opened the inner door. Then, he thought to himself, it he closed the door again, maybe the shield would go back down.

He dragged the pod inside, along with the lit box, and prepared to close the door. His frozen friend, still floated in the room as always. As Roberts grabbed ahold, he repeated the process from before, and placed the dead lifeform's hand on the pad. The light came on, and the door began to close.

Roberts held tight to the pod and box, as the atmosphere of the room vented into space. With the shield gone, everything that was not bolted down, was dragged forward. Roberts watched, as the frozen dead crew member flew past him, and out into open space.

Inside the shuttle, Allen was running random checks on the system. He was finishing, as he heard a clanking sound, on the outer hull. He looked to the sides of the ship, but saw nothing. Then, he turned to the front of the ship, just as the dead body floated just outside his window. Instantly, Allen let out a scream, that blasted through his com system.

"Allen, are you alright? What's going on back there?" Roberts, was almost sure what he had seen.

"Steven, there is a dead alien outside the ship. It is big and very frozen."

"I know, he was what hit me from behind over here. He was sucked out of the ship, when the shield went down. Pretty intimidating, huh?"

"That is one way to describe it. Where are you now?"

"Just look out to your left. I am approaching the ship now."

As Roberts came closer, Allen could see the large cryo-pod flying to his side, and in his other arm, a glowing box. He could not believe his eyes, but what could he believe after coming alongside a huge space ship in earth's space.

Allen opened the cargo bay doors, for Roberts to come inside. He activated his jet pack to guide him in, and land as carefully as possible. His descent, was a bit crude and awkward, but he had never attempted landing with a pod in tow before.

As the doors closed, Allen stabilized the oxygen in the hold. After running checks of the cargo area, he began a decontamination cycle. He wanted back inside the bay, but realized everyone's safety was at risk. The following thirty minutes seemed like a lifetime, and when it was done, Allen was on his way in.

"Steven, I am so glad to have you back onboard. You had me going there for a while."

"I am fine, and the cargo seems to have made it here safely as well." Roberts said, as he pointed to the woman in the pod.

"She really does look human. How is this possible, that she is on a ship like that. The thing has to be thousands of years old, yet she looks like she went to sleep yesterday." Allen spoke, as he studied the woman.

"You think that is cool, look at this." Roberts said pointing at the glowing box.

"Any idea what it is?"

"No, I am hoping it is an energy source. Maybe it would bring us a bit forward in the space race."

"Man, that would be cool. But for now, we have to get that war machine, moved out of its course, or the space station is toast?" Allen seemed edgy, as he encouraged Roberts to go towards the flight deck.

As they settled in their seats, Roberts fired up the engines and swung the shuttle around facing the spaceship. He studied the craft, as it floated in front of him. He wished there was some way to save it. There was no way possible, to stop the decay of its orbit in the time they had left.

"You ready for this?" Roberts asked.

"As I will ever be." Allen answered, as the laser blasted out of the front of the shuttle, aimed at the explosive pack Roberts had left in the opening of the ship. Filled with high level explosives, the blast pushed back into the ship, and caused a chain reaction.

As the ship began to explode, Roberts backed the shuttle off to a safe distance. The chain reaction moved the ship away from the space station. They had accomplished their goal, and retrieved what they believed to be important alien tech.

As the shuttle spun around and moved towards the International Space Station, the box held deep within the shuttle's cargo bay, began to flash brighter with the explosions. While inside the cryo-pod, the rescued life form blinked her eyes, and breathed deeply, as she let out a scream.

Chapter Seven ☣ Out Of The Past

As the shuttle drifted across the sky, Roberts watched the enormous wreck of a ship, moving into a new orbit. He felt the relief in his chest, as he watched it move outwards away from the space station. He knew their mission was a gamble. He was prepared for defeat, but not the loss of life.

As he maneuvered the shuttle alongside the space station. Inside, he saw the Russian cosmonaut named Pavel, waving to him through the Lab nadir window. Roberts flashed him a peace sign as he started to check the shuttle systems for reentry.

"How's our passenger back there?" Roberts asked, as Allen returned to his seat.

"Honestly, I have no idea. Cryogenics is not my field. I do know however, that the box back there is pulsing and lighting up like a disco ball. Something about it is not right. Oh, and get this, I was looking at our passenger, and I swear it looked like she was breathing."

"Tony, you know as well as I do, that girl is at least a thousand years old. Everything on that ship was ancient…to them. To think about it, their tech outshines ours, and it was obsolete a millennium ago. There is no way she could ever be brought back. There has to be some kind of time limit on cryo-sleep."

"Look Steven, all I know is, she looked like she was breathing. I don't care how long she has been asleep; you are judging her lifecycle in that chamber by our technology. They may have had a better understanding of the concept than us. She may still be alive in there somehow." Allen was not backing down from his ideas.

"Ok, you win. Maybe she is still alive, but she is still frozen. There is no way she could show signs of life from inside that pod. It is working, and she is icy."

"Ok then, we are in a holding pattern until our planned return. Come back with me and do a walk through the storage bay." Allen insisted.

"Alright Tony, if it makes you happy, I will walk with you. You know, you are more worrisome than my wife was. And you know how that ended up."

"Yeah, I seem to remember, she divorced you." Allen said, as he smiled at his friend.

They walked back to the door of the large storage area. Looking through the window, everything looked as locked down, as when they last left it. Just as Allen placed his hand on the handle, he heard a noise from within.

"What was that?" He asked.

"Tony, don't start. It was probably a piece of space junk, hitting the hull of the ship. Now, calm down and open the door."

"Steven, that was not a noise from outside. It was from the storage area."

"Open the damn door, and we will see if there is anything moving around in there." Roberts said angrily.

As Allen opened the door, he looked inside quickly, before entering the room. Roberts watched him, wanting to laugh for how silly his friend looked. From behind, Roberts shoved Allen forwards, and forced him to shoot into the room.

"Now, do you believe me. There is nothing going on in here." Roberts insisted, as he turned to leave.

Just as his foot hit the doorframe, the sound came forward again. A thumping sound, filled the room, almost like the banging of metal. Roberts stopped in his tracks, and turned to look at Allen. He moved back inside, as a muted scream echoed through the room.

Allen backed up to Roberts, and stood beside him. Neither knew what to make of it. Their passenger should have still been frozen, but the sounds came from her direction. The two moved forward, and studied the pod, which seemed to have moved across the floor two feet.

"Steven, that isn't where we left it. Look on the floor. There are scrape marks."

"Yeah, I know. Something is going on here. Look at the glass, it is no longer icy. This unit is defrosting." Roberts said, as he worked up the nerve to move over to the glass, to see inside.

As he leaned into the direction of the pod, he stared at the woman. To his surprise, she was breathing. As he came closer to touch the now defrosted glass, he watched her, as her eyes flew open and she screamed.

Roberts fell backwards, he was totally taken off guard. Allen reached down to help him up, still watching the woman. She was alive, and her eyes searched the room in fright. The more excited she became, the more the box lit up.

"What do we do now? We can't just leave her in there." Allen said, swallowing hard.

"We need to radio home base, and get their ideas on this. She could be contaminated, or worse."

"Understood. You hit the radio, and I will stay here, and make sure she does not get lose. Steven, just make it fast, I don't like this at all. For some reason, I feel like something bad is going to come of this." Allen stood his ground, as Roberts ran for the communications panel.

Chapter Eight ☣ She's Alive

As Roberts relayed his information to ground control, he knew their reply was not going to be good. No one had ever dealt with anything similar to their situation before. He sat and waited, for the top scientists on hand, to decide a course of action.

"Roberts, we talked this through, and honestly there is nothing you can do, but bring her back. We recommend you do not let her out of the pod, or give her access to the shuttle. If she is contaminated, she may infect or kill you, before you could home. Not to mention, we do not know her mental state, or if she can even communicate. Our main concern is the box. We think it has revived her, and if that is the case, it has power we do not understand. You two have to be careful, and get back here, so we can assist you." The commander's voice faded, as the screen went black.

Roberts turned and headed back to the storage area, moving quickly through the ship. As he flew through the door, he could see the woman pushing her hands against the glass of the pod. He stopped for a second, and stared at her. She was panicking. She wanted out.

As he walked up behind Allen, he made eye contact with the woman, who stopped and looked at him. He wanted to communicate with her, but he was not sure if she was capable of speaking any language, let alone English. He stopped just behind Allen, and put his hand on the man's shoulder.

"They want us to leave her in there, and bring her back for study. They are scared of us being infected, by anything she might be carrying. I am not sure if I agree, but we cannot contaminate ourselves or the ship."

"It's cruel to leave her in there like that. Isn't there any way we can scan her for contamination?" Allen asked.

"Yeah, we can use medical scanners, to get a general idea of what she may have been exposed to. And what if we find something? I mean, we retrieved her, and if she is contaminated, are we just supposed to eject her into space?" Roberts grew angry.

"That's not our decision to make. The scientists have to make the call. If we get her down to the surface, maybe they can isolate her, until they know more."

Roberts turned to look into the woman's face. "Look, I don't know if you can hear me, or if you even understand. We are not here to hurt you. We want to help. If you can wait a little while longer, we will get you to a place, safe for you and us. Do you understand?"

The woman lowered her head, and looked calmer than she had before. Allen wondered what was going through her brain. He was sure she was human. He just did not know what time in history she came from. He had heard of alien abductions, and often wondered if he believed. The government had covered up so many, but what happened to the abductees.

As he studied her, he hoped for the best. If she did come from the past, the earth she was going back too would be a very different place. He wasn't sure if a primitive could make the adjustment. For now, there was nothing he could do, but lock down the storage compartment and ready the ship for return.

As they walked away, Roberts turned and looked at the woman. She stood there in her chamber, as naked as she was when he found her. He raised his hand to wave to her, mostly out of habit. She watched him, and raised a hand to the glass. It was as if she understood.

Roberts and Allen returned to their seats, and began the process to return to Nasa. Neither said much as they went about their routines. They didn't even make eye contact for the longest time. Allen grew more and more upset at the situation. He felt what they were doing was wrong.

"Look, I don't usually rock the boat. I do as I am asked, by our illustrious government. And No, I do not always agree. This time, it bothers me. That is a living breathing person back there. What if they decide she is contaminated?"

"We do as we are told. It isn't just about her. We could be infected and die. We could spread any number of deadly germs to the general population. Remember what Spock said, 'The needs of the many, outweigh the needs of the few, or the one.' Sadly, in this case, it is true." Roberts finished speaking and closed his eyes to alleviate the headache he had acquired.

"In this situation, you quote Star Trek. I get it, I just don't feel good about it." Allen said in a half whisper.

"I hear you, let's just get ready to go home."

The engines fired, as the shuttle spun around, and prepared to reenter the earth's atmosphere. The two astronauts were quiet, as the voyage home began. In the cargo hold, the alien box pulsed faster and more brightly, until the whole area filled with light.

The shuttle began to bounce and shake, as it bounced through a turbulent atmosphere. Roberts checked the controls; he did not understand what was happening. The bouncing caused the pod to flip back and forth, until it finally landed on its side, and the outer door opened. From within, the naked woman stood up, in a brilliant light show.

As she became upright and extended her arms, the bright light engulfed her. Unknown to the astronauts, she made her way to the door and flung it open. Walking forward, her body lit the ship, with an orange-red glow. As she entered the crew compartment, Roberts turned his head to her. A blinding light filled the room, as the two men passed out.

From the communications receiver, the sound of the ground crew echoed out. "Roberts! What is going on up there. The energy readings in the shuttle are off the charts. We witnessed a bright light through the camera system. Someone, answer us. Are you still alive. Please respond."

The woman moved forward, with a wicked smile on her face. She was free. Nothing could contain her now. The whole time, the shuttle bounced through the atmosphere, and the alien box glowed brighter and brighter.

Mullins

Chapter Nine ☣ Heat Of The Moment

The shuttle bounced through the atmosphere, while the exterior glowed a bright red. On the floor of the crew area, Roberts and Allen were shaken back and forth, like rag dolls. Neither aware of their situation, or able to do anything about it. The woman stood, looking forward through the windows, as the ship made its way towards the surface.

The box pulsed, and the woman watched it, almost as if she was receiving intelligence. She was aware of the situation, and did not want to die. The pulsing of the box became rhythmic, as if it was sending the woman instructions.

She moved to the pilot's chair, and took ahold of the controls. The box, loaded the information she needed to fly the shuttle, into her brain. As she maneuvered the ship, it leveled out and returned to its planned reentry.

After she had the ship locked onto its planned course, she turned to the men. She studied Roberts, and then Allen. She was not sure of Roberts; he was not kind to her before. Then as she looked to Allen, she remembered him defending her. A smile crossed her face, as she looked at him. In her diminished mental state, she found him attractive.

Reaching out, she ran a hand over Allen's cheek. She found it to be soft. She enjoyed touching him. There was an attraction to this man, and she was aware of that much. Still, her mind was so cloudy.

As she sat on the floor, she stroked his hair, and tried to remember her life from before. Being asleep for the extended time in the chamber, had sent her into some strange mental state. She became frustrated, the harder she tried, the worse her head hurt.

Opening her mouth, she tried to speak, but no words came. She was sure, that once she had a language. She wondered if in time her mind would return to normal. She wasn't sure of anything at that point, except she was scared.

The shuttle shook back and forth a few times, and she became scared. She knew the men were the ones to fly the ship. One of them had to wake up. She shook Allen, but he still laid there in his unconscious state.

Then she turned to Roberts. She did not know what to make of him, but she was sure she did not trust him. Pulling a hand back, she slapped his face, in a way to get his attention. It worked, and he let out a groan of pain.

"What the hell was that for?" He asked, as he slid his hand to his cheek without thinking about it.

The woman tried to speak again, but all that would come out was a gasping sound. Roberts stared at her for a moment. As he tried to sit up, he felt the searing pain race through his temples. He had been hit hard, and his head told the story.

"Wait, you did this. You let loose with some sort of power surge, and knocked us both out. What the hell do you want from us?" Roberts screamed.

The woman drew back in fear, and shook her head as if she knew what he meant. In an instant, she did know. Her brain was resetting itself. She heard the sounds, and knew what they were. Then she threw her hand out, and pointed to the box.

"Why are you doing that? What does the box have to do with this?" He asked.

The woman grew angry, and repeatedly threw her hand in the direction of the box. Roberts sat there on the floor, and looked at the object, which no longer pulsed. Then he looked at the woman, who struggled to get her message to him.

"You are trying to tell me the box was doing all this? How is that even humanly possible?" He said, under his breath.

Then he realized, this was not humanly possible. The box, this lifeform and everything floating in space was alien. This was not on human terms. Then he looked at the woman, and finally understood what she was trying to say to him, since the minute she woke up in the cryo-chamber. The box was dangerous.

Roberts finally gained his balance and could focus again. He turned around, to see the ship was under control. "Did you do this? We are safely headed home. But how did you know to do any of this?" The woman did not answer, she simply pointed to the box.

Roberts turned around to Allen, who still lay unconscious on the floor. He scrambled to his friend's side, and checked the man's pulse. Roberts was relieved to find he still had one. Pulling out a medical kit, he opened a packet of smelling salts and ran it under Allen's nose.

Allen gasped for air, as he tried to raise his hand, and wave away the harsh smell. He coughed, as he tried to breathe deeply. As he opened his eyes, he saw the woman standing there. He jerked back in fear, as he realized where he was.

"What is happening? Why is she loose?" Allen screamed, as he tried to back away.

"It's alright, she is harmless. She woke me up, and got the ship on course."

"What do you mean, she did it?" Allen was confused.

"We have been out cold for some time. She woke me up after they took care of everything. Apparently, the box tapped into her brain, and gave her a crash course in shuttle flight. After that, I woke up and revived you. She thinks the box is dangerous."

"Oh, she thinks. How the hell do you know what she thinks?" Allen snapped at him.

"Because, I told him." The woman spoke from behind them.

Chapter Ten ☣ Crash Landing

"Wait, did she just talk?" Allen asked.

"Yes, I believe she did." Roberts answered.

"How…How does she know how to talk?" Allen asked.

"I think we need to ask her that." Roberts said, turning to the woman. "Let's start by asking what is your name?"

"I don't really know. My memories are scrambled by the time I spent in the chamber. I have tried to remember, I just cannot.

"Well, we will need to call you something. For now, I will call you Nova." Roberts said, smiling at her.

"Why Nova?" She asked.

"Well, back in the old days, there was a wonderful science fiction movie called 'Planet Of The Apes.' I always loved that one. The main character, became stranded on a planet ruled by apes, who enslaved humans. When the man and his astronaut friends were captured, they were put in a place to be examined by the apes, and Taylor, the lead man was put in a zoo like cell, with a human woman. They escaped the place together, with the help of two chimpanzees, name Zira and Cornelius. He named her Nova. Maybe one day on earth, I will show you this movie, and the others in the series. They made some awful remakes of the series, in the 2000s, I didn't care for them much." Roberts smiled, as he looked away from her.

"Maybe, before you do anything else, you should find her some clothing to put on. She might not mind the exposure, but when we land, she might have too much attention." Allen added.

"OK, I will find her some extra gear to put on, and you can see what our friendly little box did to the systems while we were out."

As Allen ran a check of the systems, he was happy to see everything was pretty much as it should have been. The he scanned the outer hull. He zoomed in to the landing gear. As he looked at the nose of the shuttle, something had wedged itself into the covering of the landing mechanism. He looked hard at the shape of the object. He knew this one well. It happened when the hard frozen body of the alien floated out of the alien ship.

"Roberts, hurry up, we have problem up here."

"What is it?" Roberts asked, as he ran through the door, with clothes in his hand.

"The front landing gear, take a look at it." Allen said, as he moved to the side.

"That doesn't look right. Is that what I think it is?" He asked.

"Yeah, that's a wedged door, bent from the debris of the alien ship."

"What can we do to fix it?" Roberts asked.

"Nothing. We have to do our best to land like that. I'll radio ahead, and let them know we are coming in hot. Nova, get dressed and strap yourself in, you are about to experience your first crash landing."

"Hopefully, it will not be your last." Roberts added.

As the shuttle shot across the sky headed to the landing strip, on the ground emergency crews were scrambled. The surface was coated in every kind of flame-retardant foam they could find. The crews stood by awaiting the worst outcome. After preparing the ground, the trucks backed off to a safe distance, and started their countdown.

"Roberts, this is ground control. We are as ready as we can be. Just keep your nose up, and we may just get you through this alive."

"Copy that ground control. I will do everything I can. You sure you don't want us to just ditch in the ocean?" He asked.

"Negative, we want to get you out alive. Besides, we don't want to have to retire the ship. The environmentalists would have a field day."

"I understand. Just cross your fingers and think good thoughts."

"Will do. And Roberts…"

"Yes sir?"

"If anyone can do this, it is you and Allen."

"Thank-you sir. Over and out."

Roberts returned his attention to the landing strip coming up in front of them. He closed his eyes for one moment, and said a silent prayer, as he flipped the switch for the landing gear. The rear hatches opened and the gear lowered. The front flap moved slightly, and made a metal scraping sound, as it moved in and out with no success.

Inside the shuttle, an emergency alert sounded, warning of landing gear failure. Nova sat back in her chair, trying to understand the gravity of the situation. Allen turned, and gave her a half smile. "Just hold onto your seat, and we will do everything we can, to get you down safely."

The ship bounced up and down, as Roberts began to pull up, and cut the engines. When the ground came up beneath them, the rear landing gear hit the runway. Roberts held tight to the controls, as they bounced towards the emergency crew. A tear ran down Nova's cheek, as she realized the danger, they were in.

When the front of the shuttle lowered, it bounced against the tarmac, as the shuttle vibrated violently. Roberts held tight to the brakes, as the shuttle slid over the chemicals set out to protect them. He managed to slow the craft down, as it began to spin out of control towards the firetrucks, which lined the side of the strip.

As the shuttle found its resting place, an explosion came from underneath. The crews scrambled to rescue the crew and passenger, before the ship was completely engulfed in flames.

Chapter Eleven ☣ Alien Contamination

The sirens blared, as the lights flashed all around the shuttle. The crews worked quickly, to open the outer door and retrieve the crew. Allen was prepared to jump out of the door, as he saw Roberts coming quickly behind, pulling Nova along with him.

As they hit the ground and ran for safety, the ship continued to burn. A van came up behind the crew, and the doors in the rear opened, as people with hazmat suits, jumped out. Roberts looked at them in a questioning way.

"What is going on here?" Roberts asked.

"You need to come with us sir." One of the suited men said.

"I understand what you want." Roberts raised his voice. "What I asked was, why are you doing this?"

"You have been contaminated." The man answered him.

"If you are worried about Nova, we tested her, when she came on the shuttle. She had no contaminants." Allen spoke up.

"I'm sorry sir, but there is a problem here. We believe you are all carrying contamination. It was likely brought back from the alien ship."

"I was on the ship, and my suit was never compromised. Nova was clean, so what else could have contaminated us?" Roberts stopped speaking, as he thought of the box.

The men in suits, ushered them into the rear of the van, and strapped them in. Roberts looked to Allen, and then shook his head. He was sure there was more going on, than they were being told. Alongside them in the truck were guards. Roberts thought about it, why would there be guards with weapons for someone who was contaminated?

They were rushed to the facility hospital, where they were separated. Roberts, protested all the way down the hall, to the room they locked him into. Allen tried to fight back, just as a soldier hit him in the back of the head with a rifle. All Allen saw coming, was the shine on the guard's boots, as his face hit the floor.

Nova was frightened. She did not understand any of what was going on. Everything around her was foreign. She understood the words these people spoke, but not the reasoning of why she was forced into a science lab. She was locked into a sterile room, with its own oxygen supply. Standing there, she stared through the glass at her captors.

As Roberts paced back and forth, the door to his cell opened. He looked up to see Admiral Hammond, standing before him. He had served under the man for more years than he could remember. And now, he wondered how someone he knew like family, could be a part of this situation.

"Admiral Hammond, I am surprised to see you here. How is it you are a part of this?" Roberts asked. "Do you know why we have been detained?"

"Roberts, this is all for your own good. We need to separate you, from the woman you have returned with, and make sure you are healthy. We can't have you transmitting anything you picked up from her, to the general population."

"Sir, you know as well as I do, we are fine. Allen and myself never contracted anything. As for Nova, we scanned her, she is clean. No signs of any contaminate that would harm us."

"Nova?" The general said in a harsh tone. "You named her. She is not a pet or a play thing. Hell, she might not even be human for all we know. She could be an alien, pretending she was from earth. Regardless, as of now, she is in lockdown, until the government decides how to handle this situation, or her."

"General, please try to understand what I am saying. This woman is no threat, and Allen…he has done nothing wrong. I have done nothing wrong. We were sent on a mission, and did what was expected from us." Roberts pleaded with the man, but his words fell on deaf ears.

"You will be reunited with Allen in a short while. The woman, is now a secured guest of the United States government. I have a feeling; you will not be seeing her again."

"General, please…" Roberts called out, but the man turned and walked away.

Roberts looked around him, as he wondered what was really going on. The general's behavior was odd, and not his normal way of acting. Then, Roberts looked up, and saw the camera that was aimed at him. They were being watched. He was sure then, the general said what he was expected to.

As Roberts moved to the door of his confined area, he leaned into it. The door moved more than the locked should have let it. He turned from the camera, as he smiled. The general did not come there to sell him out, he came to unlock the door.

Roberts thought about the layout of the rooms, before he was ready to run. He had one chance to escape, and he had to do it right. If the general had been to see him, then he should have done the same for Allen.

Roberts grabbed a pillowcase from the bed in his room, and in a quick movement, threw it over the camera. Turning, he ran as fast as he could, out the door and down the hall, to Allen's room. He did not look back; he knew there would be little time, before they noticed he was gone.

As he threw open Allen's door, he saw the general walking away down the hall. Roberts stopped for only a second, to stare as the man turned and looked back. With a smile on his face, the general saluted him, and moved away down the hall.

"Get a move on! It won't be long until the guards are on to us." Roberts said, grabbing onto Allen, and pulling him out the door.

"They are covering this up, aren't they?" Allen asked.

"Yes, they are. And I am afraid, to cover it up, means to get rid of us as well."

"What do we do now? How do we run from the government?"

"We have to be seen, and get the word out. But first, we have to find Nova."

As they ran through the hallways, they studied each door, and where she could be. As they passed an opening, they heard the doctors inside talking. "The spore count is off the charts. How many people have been in contact with the shuttle?"

Another voice answered back. "All of the ground crew, and now this whole wing of the building. We've all been infected."

"Notify the base commander. He has no choice, but to bomb everything. We were too late."

Chapter Twelve ☣ On The Run

Roberts ran for the end of the hall, where a computer desk monitored the whole complex. He jumped the counter, and landed just behind the keyboard, as he brought up the cameras for that area. He clicked through, as fast as he could, until he found the face, he had become so familiar with.

Nova stood in her glass cell, looking frightened. She had heard all that the staff had said about the contamination, and how she had been brought back as a mistake. She was to be disposed of, and the whole situation to be erased, as if it never happened. She had only just been brought back to life; she did not want to die like this.

Roberts flew to the outer door of her room. There was a guard posted there with a rifle. As he lifted his head to turn towards Roberts, Allen came at him from behind, hitting him over the head. The man fell to the floor unconscious. Roberts grabbed the man's gun and looked to Allen.

"You ready for this?" He asked.

"Is there any other choice?" Allen responded.

"I'm afraid, not any more. We get Nova, and run.

"Set it off." Allen said with a smile on his face.

As the door blasted open, the doctors flew out of the way. Roberts raised the gun, and aimed at one of the men standing near Nova. "Open the cell, and let her out, or I promise you, you will regret it."

"It doesn't matter you know." The man replied. "It's too late, we are all infected. The base will be blown up with a nuke in minutes."

"What the hell are you talking about?"

When you came back, you brought a contaminant with you. A deadly spore. When your ship was opened, everyone you came in contact with, was infected by it. We can't stop it."

"You mean, Nova infected us all?" Allen asked.

"No, not the woman. She shows no signs of the contagion. It was the combination of the dead alien you found in space, and the box. The radiation from the box, caused the alien's body to be a host. It is probably why the ship was left in space and never salvaged. The spores were collected on your space suit, when the body collided with you. They were dormant, then when you returned with the box, you revived them, and they started to grow within the shuttle. They fed off of the energy the box produced."

"So, when we crash landed, the crew that rescued us unleashed them, and spread them across the base, person to person." Allen added.

"Yes, so take the woman if you wish. We are all dead anyway."

Roberts opened the door, and led Nova out into the lab area. She held tight to him, fearful of what she had heard. Nova looked deep into his eyes with a saddened look. She did not want to see anyone die, but she feared these people, who would erase her existence.

The three ran for the doorway, and headed out the outer doors. They had to get off the base, before the nuke was dropped. Allen found a nearby map of the facility, as well as its underground bunkers, and tunnel to the woods.

"Where is the nearest opening to the underground?" Roberts demanded.

"The flight hangar, has an entrance in the rear, behind the stairwell. The door is marked maintenance storage." Allen said, with a nasty expression on his face.

"Well, if I had to conceal something, I would put it in plain sight too. It's a hell of a way to keep people out. Let's get over there."

As they found the door, Allen jerked at the handle, and to his surprise, there was a hidden stairwell. It was right in front of a place he had been hundreds of times. For a moment, he felt silly for never knowing. Flipping on the lights to the stairs, he flew downwards with his companions coming up, fast. Roberts slammed the door behind them, hoping the blast would wait until they were far enough underground.

As they hit the bottom landing, the explosions started to sound up top, on the surface. As the explosions happened one after another, the ground shook beneath their feet. Nova fell to her knees, as she lost her balance.

The strikes were relentless, as the level above them groaned and shook, with bits of the surface falling around them. They ducked and dodged the debris, as it rained down on them like a heavy rainstorm. Many of the pieces missed their mark, but one large chunk of cement struck Allen in the back, throwing him to the floor.

"Are you alright?" Roberts called out to him, over the rumble of explosions.

"Feels like I broke something. Don't stop for me. Save yourselves. I am no good to you like this."

"Forget it, you know me better than that. I never leave anyone behind. Nova, take his arm, and I will take the other, and we will lift him."

"Can you walk at all?" Nova asked.

"I think so, if I can lean on you two." Allen tried to hide his fear, as the building above began to collapse.

"Not to scare you two, but it is time to run." Roberts said, as he saw the ceiling coming towards them.

They ran as fast as they could, at times dragging Allen, as they sprinted to the opening of the tunnel. As they arrived just feet from the opening, the building above collapsed, and rained down on top of them. Roberts turned to look for his friends, as the lights in the room dimmed, and there was nothing but pitch black.

Chapter Thirteen ☣ Wonder Twins

Stephanie and Jason arrived just outside the base perimeter, as they watched the explosions start. Jason looked on in horror, as he realized there were still people inside the buildings. He tried to look away, but could not. For a moment, it was like a hundred people cried out for help, and then were silenced.

"Did they do, what I think they did?' Jason said, with his eyes glued to the destruction.

"Yeah, they did. It's all gone. The shuttle, the people, all the ones who knew about the recovery mission. No evidence that they even recovered anything." Stephanie spoke, with a sadness in her voice.

"Let me get this right, our own government killed its own people, to stop everyone from knowing about a spacecraft in orbit, and them launching a mission there."

"Yes Jason, they wiped out everything, that proved there was life in space before us. By tonight, they will launch a campaign, that says the sightings of the ship, and even the shuttle launch, were a hoax. And all these people, died for nothing."

Stephanie stared at the fires, that burned away the last of the evidence of the buildings, that once were. She wondered if anyone had escaped. Someone had to have found a way out, she thought. She studied the area, and remembered the online database she had found.

"Maybe they didn't all die." She said, pulling out her laptop from her backpack.

"How could anyone survive this? The buildings melted." Jason mumbled, shaking his head.

"A while back, I was researching bases in this area. And I accidentally pulled up this database of ground plans, for this, and several other locations."

Jason looked at her, with a sarcastic look on his face. "You just found this database of government information?"

"OK, I deserved that. So, I just happened to hack this database, where there were ground plans for all these bases." She replied.

"And why were you looking for this information?" Jason asked.

"With the state of the world, it is good to have accurate intel. So, as I was saying before I was interrupted, the plans for this base were on there. Ah!" She said excitedly, as she pointed to the screen. "That is what is in front of us. And below, over there at what used to be the flight hangar, is where the underground entrance is."

"You mean, under all that rubble, you hope to find a door to the underground?" Jason ran a hand over his face in disbelief. "Sure, why not."

"You don't have to go. I can do this myself." She said, looking hard into his eyes. "I just kind of hoped, you would go with me."

"What if it is contaminated? I mean, what if we are exposed to some kind of virus, or something just by being here?"

"If they turned something loose from that shuttle, we are already doomed. A bombing run wouldn't erase something like that." Stephanie said the words, and already felt the sadness from the truth.

"You know, it will take super human strength and abilities, to get through all this destruction. We are not the Wonder Twins or something." Jason joked.

"I know. Just stay with me, and we will get through this somehow." Stephanie said, as she stood up, and prepared to moved forward.

As they ran into the now destroyed base, the heat from the fires, surged all around them. Jason scanned for guards, or any other living things. There was nothing, the government had done their job well. Just as they reached the remains of the hangar, Stephanie heard a sound, but was not sure what it was.

Grabbing onto Jason's arm, she pulled him behind a partial wall. She figured out what she was hearing, it was a Jeep starting up from within one of the partially destroyed buildings. The engine sounded and then revved, as if it were about to launch forward. Suddenly, a bay door fell to the ground, as the jeep flew through it.

Just feet from the crushed door, the Jeep stopped. The soldier driving, stood up and moved to the side of it. He looked out over the area at the destruction, and then he began to laugh. Stephanie listened, and thought there was something strange about his sound.

As he turned around, she got a good look at his face and skin. He glowed, not a normal looking glow, but one that had an odd hue. She continued to watch, and she stared hard at him. He did not look human anymore. He was distorted, as if his skin was changing.

"I think we now know there was a contaminant brought back by the shuttle. And he is the proof." Stephanie froze in her tracks, not knowing what to do.

Chapter Fourteen ☣ Into The Darkness

Stephanie watched as the soldier studied the area. He did not notice them, as they hid behind the wall. Jason turned to look at her, as Stephanie put a finger over his lips, and shook her head no.

After several minutes, the soldier got back into the Jeep, and headed through a clear path in the rubble. He made his way to the main gate, where he drove through the guard post. The blockade had no effect on him. He was on his way out into humanity.

"That is what it looks like, when a contaminated person starts a chain of infection. Wherever he goes, this germ or whatever will spread. And you thought a pandemic was bad." Stephanie tried to imagine the scale of infection, that was to come.

"Are we all going to die?" Jason said timidly.

"I don't know, but if we find the crew from the shuttle, maybe they have answers, or even a way to stop this. Whatever the case, I don't think this is going to end well."

Stephanie turned to what would have been the back of the building. She studied the rubble, and saw a way in, that was not engulfed in fire. Looking under, she saw the door. It was still intact. Grabbing Jason's hand, she pulled him in with her.

Under the piles of concrete and metal, there was just enough room to open the door. Inside, the cool air, rushed past them. The fire did not extend to the lower level. She climbed down the stairs into the darkness.

Jason rummaged through his bag, until he found his flashlight. As he aimed it around, he could see the piles of debris, that would have been the rafters. He looked to Stephanie, and shrugged his shoulders. He wondered how anyone down there could have survived.

"If anyone made it down here, they had to be here for a reason. The only thing I saw on the diagram, was an access tunnel that led to the side of the mountain. If they got to the tunnel, they might have escaped. If not, they might be here under the destruction." She hoped they had escaped.

Moving down the stairs, they headed in the direction of the tunnel. Jason carefully navigated the metal pieces, that had fallen in every corner. He watched and listened, as they made their way towards the tunnel opening. As they got closer, a flicker of light, could be seen coming from just inside the darkened remains.

"There's the tunnel. It probably had emergency lights. If anyone came this way, they would have headed in there." Stephanie spoke, trying to find some positive in the situation.

As she began to move forward, Jason moved the light away for a moment, thinking he heard a noise. With a couple of steps, Stephanie caught her leg on a piece of the rafter, and fell to the ground.

She screamed, as she tried to free herself from the metal. As Jason turned back, his eyes grew large, as he looked just behind Stephanie, and began to scream himself.

On the ground, under a pile of wood was a head, just outside enough, that it could be seen. Stephanie pulled back in horror of the sight of the man. She shivered, standing there wondering why this all happened. Then she heard a low groaning sound, that grew louder.

"Steph, I think he is still alive. We have to get him out of there. Somehow." Jason said, as he looked around, for anything to help.

"The piece on top of him is not wedged. If we can get it up a little, maybe we can drag him out."

"I agree. See that beam?" He said pointing. "I will use it to push up, and grab ahold of him."

As Jason raised the pieced of wood, Stephanie pulled the man to safety. He lay there on the floor, as Jason tried to look at the man's face. He immediately recognized him as one of the astronauts.

"Allen, can you hear me?" Jason said, as he gently supported the man's head.

The man coughed and spit forth the dust, that had collected in his mouth and throat. "What…who are you?"

"I'm Jason and this is Stephanie. We came here to investigate the shuttle landing, then saw what happened. We figured if there were any survivors, they would be down here. Then we found you."

"Where are the others?" Allen asked.

"Who, what others?" Stephanie asked.

"Roberts and Nova. They were just ahead of me, when the ceiling caved in. "Are they alive?"

Stephanie turned to Jason, and shook her head. There was no sign of life, and no noise, other than their own conversation. As Stephanie stood up, she looked towards the tunnel. If anyone made it that far, they would be just inside the opening.

Mullins

Chapter Fifteen ☣ The Tunnel

Stephanie walked over to the tunnel entrance. She stared deep within, using the flickering light to help her see. Some of the ceiling, had caved in at the mouth of the tunnel, as well. Jason helped Allen sit up. They were sure he had bruised ribs, possibly more, but he insisted on moving.

"If they are in there, we have to find a way to get to them." Allen insisted.

"If your friends are in there, and still alive, we will help you get to them. Just take it slowly, we are not sure how bad you are injured." Jason said as he guided Allen towards the tunnel.

As they came up behind, Stephanie turned to face them. "I don't think the entire tunnel is caved in. It is just here, and it does not look like a lot of rubble, just some ceiling materials. As I was looking,

I saw there is a side door, over there. If your friends got inside, they may be safe, just stuck inside.

"We have to get the beam that is pinning the door out of there, and the roof pieces should be out of the way." Allen spoke, as he studied the area.

They worked together, and freed the beam, that held the other materials down. Little by little, they worked at removing the pieces. It took almost an hour, but they achieved their goal. Stephanie listened closely, as they prepared to open the door, but there was nothing.

"No matter what we find in there, it is out of our control. Just do not freak out." Jason said, as he reached for the doorhandle.

As the glow from the flashlight, lit the small room, Jason saw the bodies lying within. He turned to the others, and shook his head. They were there, still Jason saw no movement.

One by one, they entered the room, and Allen pushed past, to get to his friends. He fell to his knees, as he took the flashlight, and shined it towards their faces. At first there was nothing, no sound or movement. Then a sound, like a gasp, came from the bodies.

"Get that damn light out of my eyes." Roberts said angrily.

"You're alive!" Allen called out.

"Barely, the ceiling hit me in the head, as we were ducking in here."

"Is Nova OK? She isn't moving." Allen asked.

"Yes, she passed out, just after we got in the door. I tried to bring her around, but with no luck."

"I have some smelling salts in my first aid kit." Stephanie offered.

"And who are you, beautiful girl?" Roberts asked.

I am Stephanie, this is Jason. We came here to investigate the shuttle. We saw the bombing run, and figured you might have gotten out. We wanted to make sure you were safe. After seeing this place, I wasn't so sure you made it."

"Fear not, I have survived a lot worse than this. Although this was pretty bad. Thank you for coming to our aid." Roberts said, as he extended his hand to her. "Oh, I am sorry, since the pandemic, we don't do that so much anymore, do we?"

"Usually, no. But for you, I will make an exception." Stephanie said smiling.

Jason fished the smelling salts from the first aid kit, and handed them to Stephanie, who ran them across Nova's face. She tried the first time with no reaction, then a second. Then Nova raised a hand, to touch her nose. She was awake again.

"You had me scared there for a moment." Allen said to her.

"I felt bad, and then could not stay awake. I am better now though. Where are we?" Nova asked.

"Just inside the tunnel, that leads to the outside." Stephanie said, before introducing herself and Jason. "Who are you?"

"She is Nova. Which is the name we gave her, after she was found in a cryogenic tube, on the derelict spacecraft. We thought she was dead, and then she came out of the freeze, after we brought her onboard. They wanted to kill her and us, because we knew too much, about the ship she came from. Oh, and there is the possible contagion we brought back. I think they made it up." Roberts said, as he looked down to Nova, who began to sit up.

"I don't know how to tell you this, it was not a lie. There is some kind of contagion. We saw a soldier, leaving the base, before we came down here. He had an odd glow to his skin, and looked half crazed." Jason explained.

"You mean, he left the grounds?" Allen asked.

"Yes, he was in a Jeep, there was no way to stop him." Stephanie added.

"He is going to spread it, to every person he comes in contact with. They said it was a spore, that could be spread through touch. A person just needs to touch your skin, and you are infected." Roberts remembered what he had heard, while inside the science lab.

"Well, if you thought the pandemic was bad, this is going to be so much worse. This is alien. We have no knowledge or ability of how to treat it." Allen said lifting a hand to his head.

"Maybe we have a bit of an advantage." Roberts spoke, extending a hand towards Nova.

Chapter Sixteen ☣ The Light Of Day

"I don't know anything about medicine." Nova insisted.

"Maybe you do, and maybe you don't." Roberts stopped her. "You did not speak English, before you listened to us for a while, and adapted."

"Yes, but I did not do that on purpose. I had no idea, of how to do it."

"I hate to tell you this, but I think the aliens who plucked you from earth, were experimenting on you. Even in our day, there are tons of cases of people claiming to have been abducted each year. Most people, do not take them seriously, and call them nut cases. Some may be, but others are victims. I am sure the abductors, like it that way. If someone is not believable, then the aliens stay a fabrication. That way, they can keep on doing what they do, with no reprisal." Roberts sighed, as he finished speaking, feeling sorry for anyone who had been abducted and not believed.

"Well, for now, we need to get out of here, and get to a safer place to be." Allen said, as he looked down the tunnel. "I think we can get through the rest of the way. We just may have to take it slowly."

Nova grabbed onto Roberts, and helped him out of the door, while Stephanie and Jason followed. The trip would go slow, and take most of the night to walk. Allen could barely move, and Roberts was not much better, with his head wound.

By morning's light, they reached the opening. Roberts joked about the light at the end of the tunnel. In this case, it was no joke, it was mornings light shining in, and lighting their way. With the end of the tunnel undamaged, there was nothing to slow them down.

As Jason stepped out of the opening, he breathed deeply. Fresh air at last. He had never appreciated it before. They lived on a mountain, with so many more advantages, than those in a city would have. The air was clean, the streams and lakes were not polluted. The whole environment, was laid back and unrushed. He decided, from that point forward, he would appreciate his life…for a much of it, as he had left.

"What now?" Stephanie asked.

"We have to get proof of what happened, before the government tracks us down, and finished what they tried to already." Roberts replied.

"And exactly how do we do that? The base is destroyed, the shuttle blown up. There is nothing left to prove anything." Allen moaned.

"Well, we have Nova, for one thing. She is no ordinary human. She can bear proof to her age, and where she came from. Then there is the soldier, making his way through the mountains right now. You cannot deny, he is carrying alien spores. We just have to stop him, before he spreads them to too many people."

"So, we need a communications system, to broadcast the information to everywhere at once, so the government cannot stop us." Allen responded.

"How about that?" Jason said, pointing towards the upper part of the mountain."

"What is that?" Roberts asked.

"A television and internet broadcast dish. It is here to amplify signals to the mountain area, where they might not be readily available." Jason was proud of himself. He knew something before everyone else…he knew television.

"My boy, you are a genius. If they have a broadcast area inside, which I am sure they do, we can use it like the emergency broadcast system. Now, we just have to get from here, to there. Any ideas?" Roberts said, scanning the area.

"I think we are still on foot. No one ever comes this high on the mountain. That is why they used it for a military base. Not too many onlookers. Nice and private, for whatever you need to do. Like killing someone." Allen added.

As they began their long hike to the broadcast dish, they took some comfort in the fact no one was following them. They had escaped to freedom, but at what cost? Above them, a satellite rotated and aimed downward, to scan the mountain area. Moving grid to grid, it finally achieved its goal. "Sir, I have found them. The are just beyond the tunnel." The private called out, to his major. "So, they did survive. Well, not for long."

Mullins

Chapter Seventeen ☣ The Escape

The bright light shone down on the soldier, as he flew down the wooded road, just beyond the destroyed base. The sun reflected off the glowing color, he was now coated in. He had no idea what had happened to him. His memories, were clouded. All he knew was, he wanted to get home to his wife, and newborn son.

As he drove, he looked down at his hand, and stared at the glowing color, that seemed to shimmer and move. He wasn't sure if he was infected by some virus, or if he was imagining it all from overheating.

He thought back to the bombing run, and remembered seeing the planes overhead. His more recent memories, seemed to be the clearest to him. Older ones, seemed too foggy, almost as if they were fading. That thought scared him. He didn't want to lose the memories of friends and family.

As he slowed the Jeep, and pulled to the side of the road, he stared down at the dashboard and traced his steps backward to the beginning. He remembered all of it, even though he wished some of those were the memories that were fading.

As he thought, he raised a glowing hand, to his buzzcut blond hair. He was sweating more than he would normally. When he pulled his hand back, pieces of hair came with it. He looked into the mirror, and saw the places where his scalp looked burned.

'How could this have happened?' He thought back to the hours before. When the planes came towards them, a siren sounded. Someone on the base, wanted to warn everyone else. They did not know the planes were there to bomb. Everyone thought it was a routine flyover. It had to have been the shuttle landing there. It wasn't supposed to, but he thought it to be strange.

Then he thought about the bombs, as they rained down on the buildings. One by one, they exploded, until the whole area was a firebomb. He remembered diving into a stairwell, as the flames began to get to him. He thought he was safe there. He never realized, there was a contagion, or that he was infected.

The soldier sat looking off into space, until he heard the plane fly overhead. It was familiar, the sound of the jet engine, was just like the ones who bombed them. He turned to look upwards, and saw it. The sun burned his eyes, but he knew the jet was one of the ones from before.

He began to panic. He had to get away, if he stayed where he was, he was a sitting target. The tires of the Jeep screeched, as he returned to the road, kicking up dust in the process. He was determined to get out of the area.

As the plane flew over, the pilot saw the dust storm, he left behind on the road below. He looked hard at the vehicle and knew where it came from.

The pilot circled around, and flew over again. He was sure of what he saw.

"Command, this is Cleanup Flight 2. I have made a positive sighting, of the Soldier in a Jeep, that fled the base area. Requesting confirmation of actions." The pilot said, as he continued to fly overhead.

"Orders are clear, destroy all possible contaminants. Leave no survivors." The voice echoed through the radio.

"Affirmative."

As the pilot swung around again, he engaged his guns, and prepared to shoot. As he flew forward, the plane swooped down, and a rain of bullets landed all around the Jeep. The soldier swerved and tried to get out of the line of fire, by heading under trees that lined the road.

A few miles above on that same road, five travelers walked towards their destination. As the sound of bullets ripped through the air, they stopped and looked down the mountain. They did not need long to know what was going on.

"They will come for us next. I assume they saw a better target, before returning to look for us." Roberts spoke, as he wiped the sweat from his forehead, which was still covered in blood.

"We need to get off the road, and travel under the trees. They will hide us, and the plane won't be able to lock on as easily." Jason said, sounding scared.

"Only one problem, that plane is likely to have heat sensors. They will know where we are, even in hiding." Allen added.

"Then I suggest, we get moving. I don't want to stand here like a willing target." Roberts said, pointing the way, into the thick tree line.

As they walked deeper into the forest, the sound of the guns filled the air again. This time, they did not just fade away. The last thing they heard, was an explosion. Allen shook his head, as he thought about the soldier. The pilot accomplished his goal. Now, the plane would resume looking for them.

As the plane flew upwards, it only saw the Jeep explode. It did not see the soldier fly out of it, just before the explosion. He ran for the trees, and allowed the blast to hide his exit. Just after the plane lifted higher, it returned to look for the other targets. The soldier saw a car heading down the deserted road. As it slowed down, the driver stopped to see if the soldier was alright.

"What the hell happened to your vehicle?" The older man asked.

"Just got too hot I guess." The soldier replied.

"You look pretty hot yourself, you are glowing from it. My name is Harold. I was a Marine, back in the day. Can I give you a lift?"

"I would appreciate that Sir." The soldier said, as he shook the man's hand. As he looked down, the older man's hand began to glow, just as his did. He didn't understand why.

Chapter Eighteen ☣ The Broadcast

After hours of hiking, Jason pointed out the top of the huge satellite dish.   They had arrived. Jason ran ahead, and peered from around a tree. He was sure no one was there full time, but he needed to see for himself.

Running back, he met the others at the top of the trail. "There doesn't seem to be anyone there. Unless they keep a person on the inside, most of the equipment is run from a separate location."

"Good, so all we need to do it get inside, and see what we have to work with." Roberts said, as he groaned, while starting to move again.

"Will you be OK, to make it the rest of the way? You look like you have a concussion." Stephanie whispered to him.

"You are an amazing girl, and I appreciate your protective ways. The world needs more people like you, but for now, I will make it. Just slower, than I would have liked."

Jason studied the outside of the building. He looked for doors or openings. There was only one way in, and when he tried the door, it was locked. Then he made his way around, and looked for windows. There was only one, but it was partially opened.

He found a wooden pallet, on the side of the building, where deliveries had been made. Turning it on its side, he made a makeshift ladder, and climbed high enough to reach the window. As he flung his body towards the opening, he never considered what might be inside, or under his landing.

As Jason came tumbling down inside the place, he landed on top of a trashcan, which had not been emptied for weeks. As he scrambled to get free of the trash, the smell neared his nose. Then he knew, what rancid tuna smelled like.

His stomach turned, as he tried to pull everything off his shirt. He thought that after the tunnel, he stunk bad enough. This was worse. He put his hand over his nose, as he ran for the door to let the others in.

As Jason opened the door, his smell bellowed out, and into their faces. Stephanie backed up, and tried to take a deep breath, from the outdoors. She shook her head in disbelief, that things could get worse. But sadly, they had.

"What did you do?" Stephanie asked.

"I fell through the window and into the trash can. It must have had some thrown-out lunch in it."

"And you decided to wear it?' She laughed.

"Not on purpose. Trust me, I am not loving it. The good thing is, we know no one has been here a while. I just hope this place has a bathroom, with running water." Jason said, as he ran off looking at all the doors down the hallway.

"So, we are here. What do we do now?" Stephanie asked.

"We hack into the computer, and send a message out, over all channels, it has access too." Allen said, as he looked around the room.

"I know you want to tell people about what happened, but what makes you think they will believe your broadcast. I am sure the government is already on its way, to covering this up." Stephanie sounded skeptical.

"They are probably on top of this already, but I have a little something they did not count on. You see, when I was leaving, I grabbed a security disk. It shows everything that happened before the bombing. It's all on there, including discussion of our mission and the coverup." Allen said smiling.

Jason returned from the bathroom covered in water, but smelling much better. He walked over to the group, as Allen began to search the computer. He smiled, as he figured out how to broadcast his storage disk.

"Cross your fingers, I am going to upload this now, and type an introduction to explain it all. Then we broadcast."

"I hope this works, because it won't be long, before they send someone here to find us. We can't hide in here forever." Jason added.

"It has to work. If these spores are allowed to spread worldwide, the whole planet will become infected. It is like an extinction agenda. Human life will cease to exist. Cross your fingers, I am beginning to broadcast now."

As Allen finished speaking, the broadcast went live. All across the area that the satellite dish extended, receive the signal. As the message he typed appeared on the screen, the filmed footage from the base began to play. The government scrambled to block the signal, but not before the bulk of the message was aired.

Just afterwards, a disclaimer from the government went on the air, saying it was a terrorist group, trying to inflict fear on the people of the

United States. They asked that the message be ignored, and more information would follow. It was a good attempt to discredit the broadcast, but many who saw the video, started to question its authenticity.

Chapter Nineteen ☣ Outbreak

As the soldier and his ride made their way to his home, they encountered many people who were going about their everyday lives. All were innocent to what was about to happen to them. None aware of what a spore was, or how they could be contaminated. Whether they touched the hand of the soldier, or of the man who drove him, each became infected.

When the two men stopped at the local diner to get a drink along the way, the packed eatery became a breeding ground. It was just good manners for the men to shake hands. Between the soldier and the older man, they spoke to almost everyone in the place.

As they left, there was not one person in the diner, who did not have the glow. Like wildfire, the spores traveled from human to human. The changes began at a molecular level. The first sign was always the glow. Then the confusion and memory loss. It was as if the human side of the people was surrendered, as if they were a host. They became trapped on the inside; in a world they could not control. Like zombies, they watched from the inside out, without any desire to fight back. The spores, became the dominant force, controlling everything they touched.

The spores moved throughout the mountain town quickly. In such a small close-knit community, everyone knew everyone else. With every hug or kiss, the numbers grew. As parents sent their children off to school, or people went to work, the spores went with them.

After the broadcast, Roberts sat and stared at the screen. He was amused, at how fast the government started a campaign, to cover everything up. He was determined not to let them win. Not this time. He would find a way to spread their story.

Outside, the plane flew past again. It was monitoring the area, waiting for them to come into the opening. Stephanie watched from the window, as the plane flew low over the building. The pilot's flybys, were in regular intervals. She studied it, until she was sure, she could time its next arrival.

"The plane is flying by us every ten minutes. It just left the area, so we have roughly nine and a half minutes, to get out of here." Stephanie said, looking at her watch.

"Well, we know when it will be back, just how do we get out of here? We are all a little rested, but still injured?" Allen spoke up.

"There is a garage, out back of here. Maybe there is a car in it." Jason added.

"How do you know this." Roberts asked.

"I saw it, when I was falling through the window. I can run out and check it."

"Even if there is a car, we don't have the keys." Roberts said, sounding frustrated.

"There is more than one way to start a car." Jason said laughing.

"Wait, how would you know that. Just how many cars have you hotwired?" Stephanie demanded an answer, as he walked towards the door.

"I have skills, doesn't mean I use them." He smiled at her, as if he had more secrets, then he left.

"This one is your boyfriend?" Nova asked.

"Yes, I guess so."

"You should be careful. He looks one way, and is really another."

"Tell me about it." Stephanie said under her breath.

Jason made his way to the garage, all the time looking around him, to see if anyone was watching. He felt weird, as if someone was there in the woods, but he could not see anything. As he looked into the window of the garage door, he saw the SUV. He had found their way out.

Jason ran for the door of the building as fast as he could, but the sounds from the forest stopped him in his tracks. As his shoes dug into the ground, he stopped and looked back to the tree line. As he stared into the dim light, he saw them. Several people, who wore military uniforms. Jason panicked, as he felt the blood rushing through his system.

As he blasted into the doorway, he screamed. "We have another problem. There are people in the woods. Military people, who are moving this way."

Chapter Twenty ☣ Between A Zombie And A Hard Place

Stephanie looked out the window, trying to see what Jason was talking about. At first, she saw nothing but the shadows, that were cast by the waving limbs on the trees. Then she saw something else. It moved slowly, as it came into the light. She did not know what to make of it at first, then she saw one of the people come into view.

"This can't be right. They look like people from the base. But…I thought they all died." Stephanie said as she stepped back from the window.

"That doesn't make sense, how could they be here?" Allen asked, as he moved closer to look out.

Just as he leaned into the window, one of the officers jumped at the glass, causing him to fall backwards. As the others turned to look, it was clear, the ones outside were no longer human. Allen scrambled backwards, as he looked at the face in the window. He knew the man looking in at him.

"That's General Hammond. I would know him anywhere. We have known each other, for more years than I can count, but he looks so different. His skin is glowing, and his eyes are dark. He almost looks like a living dead person." Allen searched for the words, but he was too shocked to find them.

"Allen, have you gone insane?" Roberts asked. "You and I both know, there is no such thing as a living dead person. It is a contradiction in terms."

Roberts stood and walked over to the window, and looked out. Just as he did, General Hammond turned around, and looked him in the face. Robert stepped back, startled by what he saw. He studied the man's face. It was his old friend, the one who had put himself in harm's way, by freeing them from lockdown at the base. He wondered how this could be.

"He's not alive, is he?" Roberts asked. "Is this the contagion they told us we brought back?"

"If it is, then it is spreading." Stephanie said, hoping she was wrong. "We only saw the soldier leave the base. But if this man is here, how many others went out, and have found others to infect?"

"We have to get out of here. If we don't, they will infect us too." Jason began to panic.

Stephanie moved to his side, and placed her hand on Jason's shoulder. She could feel him tremble, as she moved around and placed her arms around him. She had always known how to distract him, when he was upset. This time, he was the worst she had ever seen him. He was shaken to his core.

"Jason, look at me. We are going to be alright. They are out there. We are safe in here. Unless they figure out how to build a battering ram, I don't think we need to worry so much." Stephanie finished speaking, as she looked over to Roberts. "What can we do? Will they go away or what?"

"Sweetheart, I wish I knew. I have never seen anything like this before. I would like to think they will give up. They are driven by the spores. The spores want to multiply. The people outside, are just bodies to inhabit. Who knows the level of the intelligence of these creatures."

"I want to call them Walkers." Jason said timidly, trying to fight off the panic attack, he felt deep inside him.

"Sounds like a good name for something like that." Nova spoke, as she looked out the window at the crowd, the moved back and forth looking for a way into the building. "I don't think they are without intelligence. They have a goal and a purpose. They want to infect. They are trying to grow their masses. They are focused like a collective. I wonder if their intelligence is linked somehow. That way they can work together and accomplish goals."

"If those things infect you, is there any coming back?" Stephanie said, feeling a shiver go down her spine.

"If the spores were removed, then possibly the body would return to normal. Mentally, there might be more of an issue. I hope none of us ever live long enough to find out." Nova stood watching the hands of the general, slide all over the glass, trying to look for his way in.

"I wonder how long the incubation period is, before they take over. I mean, could any of us be infected?" Roberts spoke, as he looked around the room.

"Wait, are you trying to make us think one of us is infected?" Jason began to panic again.

"No, I am not saying anything. If anyone should be infected, it would be me or Allen. We were in contact with the alien ship first. Nova is probably the luckiest of us all, she seems to be immune to all of this. That is why they wanted to test her. Hell, maybe if we had let them work long enough, and that bomber did not show up, we might have found a cure. Then none of this would have ever happened. But then again, the government wanted us all dead. Speaking of them, isn't it about time for our friendly neighborhood flyby to happen."

Stephanie looked at her watch. "Yes, he is due in two minutes. Wait, maybe we can use him to our advantage."

"What do you mean?" Roberts asked.

"If there is movement outside, then maybe the plane will use those nifty guns it has, to pick off a bunch of them for us?"

"My girl, you are a genius. We just have to stir them up, and make them be seen." Allen began to get excited at her idea.

"Maybe we can get the alarm system to go off. That should blast the whole outside with sound, and should get their attention long enough, to make them move." Jason said, looking at the console. "And maybe, if we confuse them enough, as the plane is shooting them, I can get to the SUV and get it started, so we can get out of here."

"Are you crazy?" Stephanie screamed. "You can't go out there. The siren might make them move, but it will not hold them forever. And what if they choose to follow you, and not the siren. Not to mention, the plane might just shoot you, instead of one of them."

"Steph, I love you. I always have. I would do anything to protect you. Right now, this seems the only thing, that might help us all. So please, let me do this. Someone has to get us out of here."

Jason turned from her, as he heard the plane flying towards them. Outside, the Walkers heard the noise too. They turned in unison, as they looked upwards to the sky. As the plane was nearing the building, Jason hit the emergency siren, and headed for the door.

Chapter Twenty-One ☣ Night Of The Walkers

As the sound of the siren flooded the area around the building, the Walkers turned and looked around in confusion. Above, the plane dove down, and the pilot saw the multiple figures outside the building. He was confused by the number of people there, but it made no difference to him. Any target, was a good target.

As he descended on the building, he aimed the guns on the ship at the targets, and turned loose a barrage of gun fire. The Walkers saw the bullets raining down on them, but stood still at first. They seemed to have no concept of pain or death.

As the first of the Walkers fell to the ground, the others soon learned, to survive, they had to move. Jason watched as they scattered. He was sure he was safe, as he saw the plane pull up. He opened the door, and began to run for the garage. He did not want to wait, to see if the pilot came around again more quickly.

Stephanie watched from the window. She was hardly ever scared, but now, she was frightened. She did not want anything to happen to Jason, but she knew, they had to escape the building. She kept telling herself, if anyone could make it out to the garage, Jason could.

Jason ran as fast as he could. He tried not to look back, as he sprinted for the outer garage door. All around him, the Walkers scattered, and tried to regroup. They seemed to be easily scared, but he was sure that would not last long.

As he neared the garage, he did not look at the ground, or at the tree root, that was sticking high enough to catch his foot. Just as Jason's foot went under the root, he flew down onto the ground hard. He had not felt anything hit him so hard, since he played football, and a bunch of built guys piled on top of him.

As he tried to regain the air, that was forced from his body, he tried to stand up. All around him, the Walkers turned and looked. They were aware of him. Those closest, started to move in his direction. They were no longer confused, by the siren or the plane.

Jason felt his heart beating faster and faster, in his chest, as he felt a panic attack start to move over him again. He did not want to be changed, or used by the spores. He was not willing, to be a host for an alien life form. He had plans, and they did not involve giving his life to something else.

He stood up, looked around, and yelled. "Not today. Not like this. You will not take me. I have too much to live for."

As Jason spun around, he looked for any openings he could find. Then he saw one, a place where no Walkers had closed in. He leaned forward and began to run, just as they started to close in on him.

He ducked past several hands, and even twisted his body, to get around the ones that grabbed at him. He was an amazing football player, and that day, he showed he had skills, on and off the field. He just pretended, he was keeping the ball away from them, and launched himself towards the door.

As Jason grabbed for the handle, he was so proud of himself, for fighting his fears. He did something for someone other than himself. He was able to save his new friends, and Stephanie. He threw his body through the door, as the hand of one of the Walkers, reached in and grabbed his ankle.

A tear ran down Jason's cheek, as he realized what was happening. He screamed out one word, "No!" Then, he scrambled to reach for anything he could. On the wall beside the door was an axe. He pried if from its holder, and grabbed hard to it. He sat up, as the Walker, tried to drag him back out of the door.

"No way in hell, I am going down like this!" He screamed, as he swung the axe, at the Walkers hand. With one quick movement, he severed the hand from the man, who held tight to him. As he sat up, he kicked the hand back out of the door. After, he quickly locked the door, to keep the others out, he looked down to his pants.

Jason stood there for a moment, considering what had just happened. He was not sure if he had been infected or not. The Walker touched him, but he was unsure if the spores, made their way through his pants. To him, it did not matter. He had to save the others. If he was infected, they would go on without him.

Jason made his way to the driver's side of the vehicle, as the Walkers beat on the garage doors, trying to get in. He felt his heart beat faster, as he wondered how long they would take, to get in. Once inside the SUV, he locked the doors, and went to work on jumpstarting it. He felt guilty about doing what he was, but their lives were on the line.

As the engine fired up, the Walkers made a rush on the outer door. A few made their way inside, as he revved the engine. When he changed the gears, the front of the vehicle, was covered in the half dead creatures. He thought to himself, 'Death is no escape.' Then he fired up the stereo, which was left playing a cd by Rob Zombie. 'Dragula' blasted through the speakers, as he slammed the gas pedal to the floor.

The Walkers began to fall to the sides of the vehicle, as he plowed forward. He watched, as the bodies, fell in every direction. He almost pitied the ones that fell under the front of the tires, as he used them as speed bumps. Determination was on his side, to get out, and to survive.

Chapter Twenty-Two ☣ Zombie Express

Jason spun the tires of the SUV, as he flew from the garage. He was scared, and pissed at the same time. He remembered the zombie movies, where they said the only way to kill them, was to shoot them in the head. At that moment, he wished he could get rid of them that easily.

As he flew around the building, the others inside watched and waited, for the moment they could run for the door. Many of the Walkers were down, after the plan had shot them. There were still a few, walking around the outside, as if they had no direction. It was those, that worried Stephanie the most.

Jason drove circles around the building, plowing down as many of the Walkers as possible. He was getting tired of playing with them. He had a mission, and they were in the way. Something inside of him had gone commando. He felt the drive inside to save his friends. He also had the fear that he was already infected. It was the only thing, that slowed him down at that moment.

After two laps of the building, there was a clearing in the Walkers, and Jason pulled up as close to the door of the building, as he could. There was barely enough room to open the door, for the ones inside to climb in over the seat. Jason smiled, as he realized he had done it. They were safely inside.

As soon as the last person sat down, Jason gunned the engine, and flew out of the driveway. A smile crossed his face, as he pulled onto the highway, and flew out of the area of the building. As he drove, the familiar sound of the plane, filled the air. It was back, and flying the path of the road.

"Oh great. What the hell do we do now? He will be shooting at us in minutes." Jason moaned.

"How good of a driver are you?" Roberts asked.

"Pretty good. I have been driving, for a few years now. Why do you ask?"

"How good are you with mountain roads?"

"I grew up here. I learned on these roads." Jason answered.

"You ever fly down them, when your parents aren't around?"

Jason lit up, and smiled at him. "Yeah, quite a few times."

"Then, it is time to do it again. Go for it."

Roberts had barely finished speaking, before Jason hit the gas pedal. The SUV's engine kicked in, and they began to fly around the curves, and cliff lined mountains. Nova grabbed on to her seat belt in fear, as the vehicle bounced back and forth. Stephanie just sat back and enjoyed the ride, she had faith in Jason's driving, she only worried about the plane that was closing in on them.

As the plane came in closer, Jason looked out into the side view mirror. He could see clearly how close the plane was swooping down towards them.

As the bullets began to fly in the direction of the SUV, Jason began to swerve. He was determined to survive this fight. He didn't give up for the Walkers, and he sure wasn't going to do it, for a man in a plane.

Jason studied the road ahead. He needed some place, to get out of the pilot's sight. Even if it was a covered bridge or whatever. Then he saw it, his salvation, a sign for the tunnel up ahead. He only had to make it another six miles, and then they were away from the plane's bullets.

The lack of traffic on the road, allowed Jason to swerve from side to side, making it hard for the pilot to fire on him. The pilot tried to match his moves, but Jason's erratic driving made it impossible. His driving, was as good as his football run on the Walkers. He had finally found the things that made him valuable to the group.

"You are doing an amazing job keeping us alive my boy." Roberts called out to him, from the back seat.

"I'm just doing what I have to do. I have this desire to live. I would love to see 21. I won't get there. if I let someone kill me." Jason said, looking back in the review mirror.

"Just keep up the good work. You have a plan for where we are going?" Roberts asked.

"Yes, I do. Up ahead is a tunnel. If the plane's pilot wants to chase me in there, he is welcome. Though, I wouldn't recommend it. Might be a tight fit." Jason laughed at his words.

As Jason glanced back, he saw the plane diving in quickly. Jason smiled, as he saw the opening of the tunnel. He was paying attention in both directions at once, something he did not think the pilot was doing.

As the mountain came up fast in front of them, Jason floored the gas and whispered. "Come on baby, give me all you got." And the SUV went into overdrive, and shot forward. The plane moved down in pursuit, and did not see the rock formation, closing in front of him. Jason shot into the tunnel and slowed down, as he heard the explosion form the outside. He settled back in his seat, realizing he had won the race.

Chapter Twenty-Three ☣ The New Locals

As the SUV flew out of the end of the tunnel, Jason let up on the gas. It wasn't far, until he reached the town, and he knew the road in was a speed trap. He did not want his first ticket, to be because of a high-speed chase. That would hard to explain to his parents.

Just outside the town area, Jason looked around as he drove. Something had changed there. Usually, there were people everywhere. There was always something going on, but today it seemed deserted. He kept looking for people, anywhere, but there were none.

"Steph, notice anything wrong?" Has said, motioning out of the windows.

"Yes, I see what you mean. Something is different here. The streets are never this deserted. Where could everyone be? I don't like this."

Stephanie tried to imagine any reason for the absence of people.

"Could the Walkers have made their way here?" Jason tried to make sense of it.

"Maybe not the Walkers in general, but maybe one did. Remember the soldier from the road. If he hitchhiked, he would have been here hours ago." Allen was scared by his own words.

"If he has been here, and passed the spores to whoever picked him up, and they ran into other people…Then this whole place can be contaminated by now." Roberts interrupted. "Whatever you do, don't stop for anyone, even if you think you know them. At this point, we have no idea what is going on."

As they passed through the town, the roads were all empty. It seemed everyone left in a hurry for some reason. Jason drove through the main streets, trying to see if he could find anyone still there. Then as he rounded the corner to the court house, he saw more than he wanted to.

In park, in front of the court house, hundreds of townspeople stood in a group. In front of them was one man, who looked like he talking. Stephanie studied them, looking for familiar faces. In the crowd, they all seemed to have the same glowing skin. Many were in different stages of infection, all looking as contagious as the others.

Stepahanie looked hard through the faces, until her heart beat faster. In the center of the crowd, her parents stood there, like lifeless zombies. She let out a gasp of air, as she felt her stomach begin to turn. She knew at that moment; she had lost them.

Jason looked up, when he heard her make the noise, then he too saw them. He reached a hand back to her. He knew there was nothing they could do. There was no stopping or reasoning with them. Then he thought, they were just like the Walkers he had killed earlier with the SUV. They were someone's family once too. He almost felt bad about his actions, then he realized, they were in a kill or be killed situation.

They crowd all turned in unison, as they saw the vehicle. It was as if, a message was sent through their shared consciousness. As a group, they started to move towards the SUV. Jason swallowed hard, as he put both hands on the wheel, and pushed on the gas pedal.

"I am so sorry Steph. We can't save them, but we also cannot allow them to capture us." Jason tried to explain his actions.

"No, I understand. We have to live to get help, and maybe one day we can save them. Or maybe not. I just hope we find a way to reverse this. I just have a feeling; this is only the beginning."

Nova looked back out of the rear window, as they drove away. She felt guilty for what was happening. She felt if she had not been rescued from the ship, then none of this would have happened. The people who had died, were on her conscious. She wondered if her immunity might be a lead to a cure.

"You have been very quiet." Allen said, looking at Nova.

"You should have not come to the ship. If you had left me there, none of this would have happened."

"Don't be silly, you did not start this. Even if Roberts had not brought you back, we still might have encountered the spores. The box activated them, I am sure of it. Don't blame yourself, for something you had no control over."

"I really wish you were right. Just deep down inside, I don't know." Nova turned from him and returned to the window.

As they drove away, Jason looked at each street he rolled by. He searched for people and faces, he looked for his parents. They were no in the crowd at the courthouse. He wondered if they were changed like the others.

After what happened with Stephanie, he didn't dare open his mouth. She was suffering enough. He just sat there in silence, and looked down to his leg, where the Walker had grabbed him. His mind wondered to all sorts of places, but mainly, if he was going to turn into one of them.

Chapter Twenty-Four ☣ The Power Of Fear

As the vehicle arrived at the next town, Jason watched for any sign of people. There didn't seem to be anything out of the ordinary. He slowed down, as he neared the diner two blocks in front of him. People seemed to be coming and going as normal.

"I don't think they have been changed yet. They all look kind of normal. Maybe the outbreak is contained back home." Jason said, as he studied the people leaving the building.

"Perhaps, but we still need to be on guard. I think we need to find a place to clean up and get some normal clothes, so we don't stick out as much." Roberts was aware, they were still wearing their flight suits, and Nova had on the scrubs, the scientists had given her.

"There is a motel up the road. We could get a room. Jason and I could go out, and buy some new clothes, while you have a chance to clean up. Oh, and take care of the blood you are covered in." Stephanie spoke, as she ran her eyes over the blood stains, she had not had a chance to see before.

"Fine, let's do that. I have money in my wallet. Should be enough for clothes and the room." Allen said, as he handed his wallet to Stephanie.

As Jason went in to pay for the room, the others stayed behind in the car. They did not want to alarm anyone with their appearance, or have to explain how they got that way. When Jason returned, they all moved to the room quickly, as to not allow anyone to see them.

Roberts headed for the shower, as Stephanie and Jason headed out to the stores down on main street. As they walked, Jason was unusually quiet. His mind was on his leg, he was sure he was infected. He just did not see any sign of it yet. Jason hoped he was wrong.

"Ok, you have never been this quiet in your life. Spill it, what is wrong?"

Jason looked up from studying his leg. "I'm Ok, just a lot to take in. I mean, I did not see my parents, and you did see yours. So many people we knew are now infected by this contagion. I just don't know what to think. What happens if this continues to spread unchecked? Will we all become infected and worse, will people die from it?"

"I don't know. I am scared for my parents, and everyone for that matter. What happens if one of us gets it? You, are all I have left. I don't want to be on the run from this on my own." Stephanie breathed deeply, as she felt a lump forming in her throat.

"We're going to get through this together. I will do everything I can to protect you. Besides, Roberts and Allen seem to be knowledgeable about staying alive. Hell, they went to space, and entered an alien ship. Still, they are here." Jason tried to make her believe they had a chance.

"I guess you are right. Ok, we fight the good fight, and stay alive. For now, we have to get these people some clothes."

Inside the local department store, they moved from women's to men's clothing, and found everything they thought would be needed. Jason was traumatized by the trip through the bras and panties. Stephanie just laughed at him, and told him to grow up. Still, they found everything they needed.

After they paid, Jason looked over to the grocery store on the corner. They had never considered food. He grabbed Stephanie's hand, and dragged her towards the doors. He just looked at her, and smiled as he said, "People have to eat."

As they returned to the motel room, Stephanie slid the card, and bounced open the door, while her arms were filled with bags. She started to let out a scream, as she looked up, and saw Roberts naked. Except for a towel, he wore nothing, as he was aiming a gun at her. She stopped dead in her tracks, as Jason gasped for air.

"I'm Sorry." Roberts said quickly.

"What the hell are you doing? Trying to give me a heart attack?" Stephanie forced the words out.

"No. It's just the way you came through the door, I thought we had been discovered."

"Not really, just my arms were full of bags." She shook her head, as she laid the bags on the bead nearest the door.

"I see you found what you went after." Allen said, as he entered the room, trying to hide his body under the towel that hung off him.

Stephanie handed him his wallet, and began to hand clothing to the both of them. "Where's Nova?" She asked.

"She just jumped in the shower as I left. Wow, you guys did great. You got the sizes right and everything." Allen said, as he started to slip on the clothing, as modestly as possible.

"You two have been great. We do appreciate you, and all you have done to help us through this. And, we would understand, if you didn't want to go any further." Roberts struggled, trying to find the right words.

"Like it or not, we are in this for the long haul. We can't go home, and hell, we have already been shot at, chased by infected zombies, been in high-speed chases, been through a military bombing. How could it get worse." Jason asked.

"Oh, it could get worse. The government could kill you, or worse, you could become one of those not so friendly zombies." Allen spoke from the back side of the room.

"We all have to die sometime. Just not now, I hope." Stephanie made a face, as she forced her fears down deep inside, and began to sort through the food. She handed out a few things to the men, as she turned towards Jason. She was sure there was something he was not telling her. If he was hiding something, it has to be bad. And then, her mind raced to the worst thing she could imagine. He was infected.

Chapter Twenty-Five ☣ Government Cover-up

For a moment, they all let their guards down, as they settled into their new clothing and food. It was a time for much needed rest. Allen rested his head on a pillow for just second, before he was asleep.

Jason looked back to him, and looked to Roberts. "He must have been exhausted."

"I think we all are, but he has had it worse. I am sure the ceiling that caved in on him, did damage. He is just too brave, to let on how badly he was hurting. How about my boy? You have had a lot thrown at yourself and Stephanie. You two holding up Ok?"

"Yeah, as good as we could be, in these circumstances. It is kind of like a Sci-Fi movie or something." Jsaon laughed.

"Well, since we are on the subject." Stephanie moved over to look him in the face. "What are you hiding? I know you are holding something back, and I think I know what it is. So, own up, what happened to your character in this movie?"

"What are you talking about?" Jason tried to hide his deceit, but she saw right through him.

"You're infected, aren't you?" Stephanie yelled at him.

Allen flew up from his dead sleep. "What…what's going on?" He asked.

"Damn it Jason, just tell the truth, and stop acting like a scared rabbit, jumping every time we see an infected person."

"Ok, I was going to have to tell you eventually." Jason hung his head in shame. "Back at the satellite dish, when I went to get the vehicle, I was attacked."

"What do you mean attacked?" Roberts asked.

"I managed to get past all of the infected military, until I got to the garage. Then one grabbed me by the leg. I fought it off as best as I could. I got away, but it touched my leg." Jason explained.

"Wait…wait, you said it touched your leg. Did it touch your skin, or bite you?" Roberts asked.

"No, I never felt anything on my skin. Just my pants leg."

"Son, you are not infected. You never made contact with the contaminated zombie. They have to pass the contagion by skin contact. Your pants were touched, not you." Roberts laughed.

The Jason looked down at his leg. He began to panic. The zombie had touched his leg. In a feverish panic, he ripped at his belt, trying to get it unbuckled. When he finally got it open, he kicked off his shoes, and threw them to the side. In a last effort, he threw his pants down, and kicked them off, across the room.

Standing there in his shirt, and boxer shorts, he looked up to the others. His face turned red, as he realized he had exposed himself. His breathing was erratic, as he tried to form words. "The contagion was on my pants. I had to get them off."

"Stephanie, I think you will have to go back to the store, and get this boy some new pants." Allen said laughing, as he tossed his wallet in her direction. "I am going back to sleep."

As Allen drifted off again, Nova entered the room. She looked around at everyone, as she wondered what had happened. Approaching the bed, Stephanie handed her the clothing that they bought. Nova smiled, as she looked at Jason. "Nice legs." She then turned, to go back to the bathroom and dress.

As Stephanie was about to leave for the stores, Roberts turned on the television. As the sound came up, a special news report was in progress. On the screen, they showed the bombed out military base. A story came after, about how the bombing was the result of terrorists. On the screen, were images of the Roberts, Nova and Allen.

As the story continued, Roberts moved to the front of the television, and put his hand over his mouth. He was in shock. The government was attempting to throw them under the bus, to take the blame for all that happened.

"They're setting us up. Now, they won't have to do the job of finding us. Anyone we come in contact with, will do it for them."

Roberts fell back into the end of the bed. He knew they were in trouble. If the zombies did not get them, the government had made sure, the people would. He studied the screen, as the report kept going. Not a word was said about the contagion. Nothing about the infected zombies roaming the mountain town. They had been set up to take the fall.

"What do we do now?" Jsaon asked.

"We need proof. Some way to show we are innocent." Roberts said under his breath.

"Doesn't the government track things in airspace?" Nova asked, as she entered the room.

"Yes, we just have to get to a satellite tracking base that recorded our mission and reentry. They would probably have evidence of the bombing as well. We just have to get that data, and we can prove our innocence.

Chapter Twenty-Six ☣ The Infection Has Spread

Roberts became paranoid, as they packed up the few things they had in the room. He walked towards the window, trying not to be noticed as he looked out. As he pulled the curtain out slightly, he saw the police car, moving just outside the motel office. He knew they were in trouble, as the clerk moved outside to meet it.

"I knew it." Roberts grumbled, as he let go of the curtain.

"Knew what?" Nova asked.

"There is a cop parked right by the office. Want to guess where he is headed?"

"How can that be, the report just hit the TV news?" Jason started to get nervous.

"It doesn't take long I guess." Stephanie said, grabbing the bags and heading towards the door. "We have to get in the car and go, before he gets a chance to come after us."

"Agreed." Roberts said, as he began to usher the others out the door.

As the cop spoke to the clerk, they quickly piled into the car. The men's backs were to them the whole time. Neither, saw as the car backed slowly out of the parking space, and rolled down the hill. The men turned to go towards the motel room door, after they escape had been made.

"I can't believe we got out of there without being seen." Jason said, with a sound of relief in his voice.

"I hate to tell you, that was nothing. The search has just begun. They will be coming for us, and they won't give up, until we are captured or dead. You kids are putting yourselves at risk. They did not show you in the search. Which means they probably do not know about you. If we are put in a situation where are going to be captured, I want you to get as far away from us as possible." Roberts could not hide the fear in his voice.

"Understood. When and if we are in that situation, then we will do as you ask. Not that it means that much, if the world is about to become infected zombies." Stephanie's voice was filled with sarcasm.

"Oh yes, and there is that. We have to find that satellite tracking station, and get the data before we are infected. Maybe then, Nova will be the possible cure to reverse this plague." Roberts said laughing. "It is as crazy as it sounds."

"So where do we go?" Jason asked.

"Just two hours south of here, is an isolated facility. It has been used for years to track broadcasts from space. They also keep data on any ships entering or leaving orbit, and government maneuvers. The good thing is, they are an often forgotten about installation. The government has never taken them seriously. Maybe now they will." Roberts finished speaking, as he studied a map pf the roads ahead, and directed Jason where to drive.

As they headed south along the highway, they studied the different roadside businesses. A disturbing trend had started to creep in, as they noticed many of the locals, were just standing outside the locations looking mindless. Jason tried to look away as he drove. He realized, he was almost one of the mindless creatures, he saw before him.

"Will there be anyone manning this place, when we get there?" Stephanie asked.

"Maybe, I am really not sure of what to expect. Being it is not a major installation; I can only imagine they have minimal staff. Perhaps one or two people on location. Why do you ask?" Roberts replied.

"What if they are infected?" She said sarcastically.

"Then we defend ourselves, and get what we are there for. Hopefully not getting infected along the way." Roberts turned toward the window, and looked out at the people who stood staring at the road. He had no desire to join their ranks.

"Uh guys…I don't want to alarm anyone, but there is a police car, coming up fast. It looks like the one from the motel. What do I do?" Jason asked.

"Gun it, and don't let up, until we shake him." Allen called out.

Jason hit the gas, and flew as fast as he could down the road. He had driven fast many times before, but never with the police in hot pursuit. This

time it was not fear of being caught, it was fear of
being captured

Chapter Twenty-Seven ☣ The Spread Of The Plague

Jason held tight to the wheel, as he pushed the SUV as fast as it could go. The cop car, hung tight behind him, as they raced down the deserted road. Jason tried everything he could think of, to get away but nothing seemed to work.

As the police car came closer, Jason stared through the rear-view mirror. Each time the police car sped up; Jason focused on the man's face. Something was not right, and he knew it. Then he saw what he was looking for.

"That police officer, is contaminated." Jason yelled out.

"How do you know?" Allen asked.

"He is glowing. I wasn't sure at first, but when the sun hit his skin, I saw it."

"Then the contagion, is spreading faster than we thought." Allen's face turned grim, as he looked out the window.

"So, what do I do about the zombie cop behind us?" Jason began to panic. "He is not going to give up."

The next side road you see, fly onto it as fast as you can, without flipping us." Roberts said studying the map. "I will try to get us onto a side road, and maybe lose him in the process."

They flew down the road, as Roberts looked for their escape. Ahead, was a dirt road, that led to an area where timber had been removed. Just then, Roberts smiled, as he realized they had the advantage.

"Jason, if you can get us off this road fast and onto the dirt road, we can use the side road where the timber has been cut. The police car cannot make it through rough terrain like we can. This baby has all-wheel-drive. Time to put it to use." Roberts began to smile, as he found their advantage.

"I'll have to slow down to do that. What if he rams us?"

"Don't worry, we will be well into the rough wooded area, before he can do anything."

As Jason saw the road coming up in front of him, he turned the vehicle as hard as he could. Flying around the corner, the two passenger side wheels left the ground, but Jason held tight to the wheel and hit the gas once again.

Behind them, the officer did not anticipate what Jason was doing, and overshot the side road. Jason let out a laugh, as the police car flew past the end of the road, and had to stop to back up. By the time it got back to the turn off, Jason had made it all the way to the wooded area.

He pulled in as fast as he could, trying to avoid the many holes gouged by big trucks, and the fallen timber that laid all over the place. He was careful but fast, which was more than the police car could manage, as it bounced through the road.

As Jason flew through the makeshift road, he saw the police car bounce higher and higher. He was sure the car was going to break an axel soon. Then he saw their salvation. Up ahead, was a deep trench bulldozed out of the road area. Jason knew if he could fly to the side of it, the police car would crash.

Jason slowed the SUV, to allow the police car to catch up with him. He knew what he was doing. He was about to set a trap. A trap that would set them free. He watched the car as it came closer, and he started to pull to the side of the road.

"Jason, are you crazy?" Stephanie asked. "Speed up and get us the hell out of here."

"Steph, you have to trust me, I know what I am doing."

"Yeah, you are about to get us captured, and turned into those zombies." She screamed.

"No, I am not. Just wait for it."

Jason hit the gas, as the police car came closer. He was sure of what he was doing, even if no one else knew it. As the SUV lurched forward, the police car closed in.   The officer stared hard at the SUV as he came close, as he should have. Jason had the advantage; he knew the officer was not paying attention to the road.

As Jason hit the end of the road, he veered right, and the SUV swung past the missing part of the road. The police car flew forward, launching into the air, and crashed front-end first, onto the embankment. As Jason watched, he could see the car's front-end crunch, as it hit the rocks in the embankment.

"You are slick my boy. You saw that coming, and used it to your advantage. That was a Duke's of Hazzard moment there." Roberts began to laugh. "Don't let anyone, tell you not to do something again."

Jason smiled, as he looked through the rear-view mirror, at Stephanie. She looked back at him, with a sarcastic look on her face. "Ok, this time you were right. Just warn us next time, so we do not think you are crazy." With that, Jason hit the gas, and began their journey through the wooded road on their way to a safer place, they hoped.

Chapter Twenty-Eight ☣ Mr. Data

From the road that led to their destination, they could see the satellites arrays, rising high above the tree line. Jason looked up, as they came into view. He was like a child, excited to see such a sight. Spread out over the mountaintop, there were eight larch dishes total. It was like a science fiction fan's dream come true.

"Just look at them. They are so huge. I can't believe the size of this place. And you said this was a forgotten installation?" Jason gushed.

"Yes, to the government, this is small and insignificant…unless they have a use for it." Allen added.

"Nova, are you alright back there? You have been so quiet, since we left the motel." Roberts could not contain his curiosity.

"I am well. There is just so much to take in.
So much I have not seen before, or understand. I
barely remember being here on earth, and what I do
remember, is nothing like this. My time was less
sophisticated and technological. I am fortunate to
have absorbed so much knowledge, while being
subjected to the alien box. I guess I am still
overwhelmed. And now, to see this, is more than I
could have imagined." Nova looked out of the
window in awe of her surroundings.

"If it all gets too much, just tell us and we will
help you through. I guess none of us thought about
what you are going through. We have just had so
much to deal with since you arrived here." Roberts
stopped, and rubbed his eyes. "I promise, we will do
better."

Nova just shook her head, as she continued to
look out at the great metal structures. Jason brought
the vehicle to a stop in the center of the grounds. He
looked at the monoliths, one by one. He did not
know where to go, being they all looked similar.

"So, we are here. Which dish, is which?" Jason said, looking at Roberts.

"The one near the center, with the larger building underneath, should be the computer operations center." He said, pointing at the building. "I guess it is time to go up and knock, and see if anybody is home."

"Yeah, I am just worried who might be at home." Allen spoke, trying to work up the nerve, to get out of the car.

"I have always dreamed of seeing a place like this. I just never thought it would be under these circumstances." Stephanie said, as she walked past the others, and moved closer to the building.

As they converged on the doorway, Roberts put his hand on Stephanie's shoulder, and stopped her in her tracks. He did not have to use words. He wanted to be the one, who faced the danger first. He was not any kind of hero, but he still felt the need to lead the group. If for no other reason, than to save them from the danger, that might await within.

As Roberts reached the door, he tried to turn the handle, and pulled at the door, but nothing happened. He then tried knocking, but again…no response. He turned to the others, and shrugged his shoulders. He thought about the situation, and did not want to commit a criminal act by breaking in, but they had already been labeled criminals.

As Roberts looked around, he saw a large rock to the side of the building. Picking it up, he returned to the door, and studied the glass. If he could smash through, he would be able to reach the handle inside. He lifted the rock in his hand, and was ready to smash the glass, when he heard a sound from behind.

"I wouldn't do that, if I were you." A man's voice echoed around them.

Roberts turned to see the man who had come from behind them, when they were not looking. "And who the hell are you?"

"I am the scientist who studies the galactic radio noise, this dish array receives. My name is

Professor Datalaine, but everyone who works with me calls me Mr. Data." The man spoke, as he came in closer. "Now, why don't you tell me why you feel the need, to break into my place of work."

"I'm sorry, we knocked, tried to the door and no one answered. We need inside, because you have proof in there, that we need to clear our names." Roberts tried to explain.

"And how could a satellite system that is made to receive cosmic noise, help you?"

"We are the astronauts from the alien craft recovery mission. Or what the government is trying to cover up. They are saying we are criminals, and that we deliberately destroyed a government base. What they are not saying, is that they destroyed their base, to cover up that they set loose a contagion, that is spreading across the area." Roberts tried to explain. "People are infected, and turning into these zombie-like creatures. If we can clear our names, maybe we can stop all this. I know this sounds crazy, but it is true. If we can track our shuttle, and the area of the base at the time we landed, we can prove it."

"I saw the news. I thought something was strange about the report. Typical government, trying to coverup their mistakes. Just like Roswell, all over again. If it has anything to do with aliens, then they try to get rid of the evidence. I know there are aliens, I have recorded the communications. I even recorded telemetry of the alien ship, and the Black Knight satellite. I have proof."

Chapter Twenty-Nine ☣ The Truth Is Out There

Mr. Data opened the door, and led them inside. In a chair near the door, he piled his backpack and other supplies, he had brought with him. As he turned to the group, he pointed to the large screen on the back wall. Reaching for his computer keyboard, he spun around and the screen lit up.

"Watch and see." He said, as he pointed the keyboard to the screen.

The file loaded, and showed tracking of the derelict ship, as it entered the Earth's air space. The movement showed the ship, as it drifted slowly downward. Then just as the ship seemed to stop near the International Space Station, another tracking signal entered the screen. It was the Black Knight, which moved in like it was propelled towards the ship. It stopped just beside the giant ship, as if it was studying it.

"See what I told you? I have proof, but no one will listen to me." Mr. Data grumbled. "Now, it you watch, the Black Knight powers up."

As they watched, the Black Knight began to position itself, as lights all around it, seemed to come online. At first, they were subtle, then they began to blink in a feverish pace. It was as if the satellite, was communicating with something or someone. Then the huge derelict ship, began to light up.

"See that, the satellite is communicating, why else would its lights be blinking? Its computer is online."

"You mean to say that satellite was communicating with the dead ship?" Allen asked.

"Not necessarily, I think the signal went beyond the ship." Mr. Data explain. "Just look at this tracking information. The signal goes past the ship and towards the moon."

"Wait, you are trying to say something on the moon, is alive and sending signals?" Stephanie said, swallowing hard.

"Yes, I believe so. And it is not the first time I tracked a signal from the moon. It has happened on and off for decades. They say, there have been signals since the 1960's." Mr. Data took a deep breath. "Did you ever stop to think, that we went to the moon, but have never gone back? What happened off camera, that we do not know about? Did they encounter something? And if they did, who or what is there, tell them not to come back?"

"That's just alien conspiracy talk." Jason insisted.

"No young man, that is based on evidence." Data turned to him. "So, you believe a space ship is in our orbit, and you believe in the alien satellite, but not alien life on the moon?"

"OK, I get your point. Why would aliens live on our moon?" Jason asked.

"Who knows, maybe they are guiding our development. Did you ever watch Ancient Aliens? They believe it is possible. Hell, a lot of scientists believe the moon is hollow. Between 1969 and 1977, seismometers installed on the Moon by the Apollo missions recorded moonquakes. The Moon was described as "ringing like a bell" during some of those quakes, specifically the shallow ones. Makes you wonder, doesn't it."

"So, you think the ship, the satellite, and the moon have ties." Nova asked.

"Yes, I do, and so do a lot of other scientists, but the government has always covered it up. Hmm, you seem out of place. There is something different about you." Mr. Data spoke, as he staired at her.

"There is a reason for that." Roberts blurted out.

"She came from the ship." Allen added.

"She is alien?" Data started to shake.

"No, we have every reason to believe, she was an alien abductee from so long ago, we have no idea. We brought her back from the ship, when we went there to investigate, and plant bombs to change its course. It would have drifted into the space station, if we did not stop it. I went onboard the ship, found her and a power device, and brought them back." Roberts grew frustrated, as he explained. "Then we crash landed at a government facility, where they discovered a contagion that traveled with us. Now, it is spreading like wildfire through the population."

"That explains the reports of a new Covid variant, that just conveniently showed up in the last two days. They are quarantining some places, and issuing travel warnings. I saw footage where the government is rounding up people, and putting them into camps. If this is as fast spreading as it looks, we better find a cure soon."

"We may have a cure. We just have to avoid the government, to test our belief." Nova spoke up.

"And what makes you think you have a cure?" Data asked.

"I am immune to the contagion. I can only believe the aliens experimented on me. I mean, after all, they made the contagion. That might explain what happened to their ship. Maybe they were trying

to find a cure, by experimenting on one of the…."
Her words trailed off."

"You mean a lab rat?" He added.

"I would not have used that term, but for what it is worth, it is accurate." Nova tired of the conversation.

Mr. Data turned back to the screen, and tracked the lift off of the shuttle. He followed it all the way to the derelict ship, and then tracked all their movement side by side, until they returned. Searching the data on file, he was able to show when they landed, and the bomber that moved in shortly after, that destroyed the base. When everything was collected, he downloaded it all onto a drive for them.

"This proves you are innocent." He said, as he handed them the drive. "I don't know who you plan to give this to, but I would hedge my bet a little."

"What do you mean?" Roberts asked him.

"Let's film an intro, explaining your innocence, then send it and the data proving your story, out to the world. I mean, they intercepted, and destroyed your first story. Let's give everyone proof, that they cannot contradict."

They prepared a video, and attached all the information. Within minutes, the file was sent worldwide, through the internet, and television to anyone who would watch. Mr. Data was thorough in his attempt to get the word out. He believed they had accomplished their goal. They were prepared to leave, with their innocence secured.

Outside the building, the black SUVs pulled up, one by one. They surrounded the building, as men and women stepped out in dark clothing, with guns in hand. They had come there on a mission, and no amount of video broadcast, was going to stop them.

Mullins

Chapter Thirty ☣ And Then There Were Four

As the door opened to the building, the sound of rifles being prepped, echoed through the open space. Mr. Data stepped in front of the door, trying not to let his fear overtake him. He raised his hands, as if to show the task force, that he was not challenging them.

"I'm not armed, and I am cooperating." He spoke, as he moved forward.

"Shut up and stand still." A female voice, called out from the crowd. "Where are the others?"

"They are not here." He said, as his knees felt like they were giving way.

"Then where do they go. We know you were with them inside. The broadcast just ended." The woman yelled back.

"They left out the back door."

Inside the building, Roberts listened to Mr. Data. He was sure his answers, were suggesting a course of action. He turned and moved to the back of the building, where he located the back exit.

Looking outside, he studied the area, and saw there was no one to be seen. He looked back to the others, and slowly opened the door. A slight creak echoed out as, as the door moved open. Roberts froze for a second, as the sound cut through the air. Then when the door was fully opened, he motions for the group to follow him.

While the task force was occupied out front, the group ran for the back of the next satellite dish. Rounding the corner, they discovered a work truck out back, and ran for it. The task force was unaware of their presence, until the truck's engine turned over.

Roberts swallowed hard, as he hit the gas. He didn't have time for second guessing. The truck flew around the building, and headed towards the road in front. The task force turned and raised their guns, as the truck flew past, stirring up dust as it went.

Roberts stomped the gas, trying to get the truck to move faster, as the raised guns opened fire on them. In the front seat, Jason pulled Stephanie's head down to his knees, trying to protect her. He used his body as a shield against anything flying in their direction.

Roberts swerved back and forth, hoping to avoid the gunfire. It might have worked, except, Allen had already taken a bullet. He fell to the side as the truck flew down the main road. Nova grabbed ahold of his head, and looked at the blood, as it coated his skin.

Nova pounded at the back window of the truck, and screamed for help. Jason raised up, and looked back. For most of the time they had been together, he had not taken this adventure seriously. The fear of being contaminated was one thing. The idea one of them could die, hit home with him.

"Allen is hit." Jason turned, and screamed.

"What are you taking about?" Roberts' greatest fear was realized.

He looked for a side road, or any place he could stop the truck, without being seen from the road. As he looked up ahead, he saw an old gas station. It was perfect, if he could get the truck in behind it before they were seen.

As the building grew closer, Roberts studied the road behind him. They had not caught up yet. He turned the steering wheel hard, as they flew around back of the building. As the truck was still rocking, he jumped out, and ran to Allen.

"Hey buddy, you alright?" Roberts asked.

"I think my luck finally ran out." Allen said laughing.

"Aww, Tony don't say that. It's going to be alright."

"Steven, you have been my best friend most of my life. I wouldn't have changed that for anything. We had the best and craziest life I could have ever imagined. I mean, how many people get to go into space with their best friend? But now...this is my last adventure. That bullet did too much damage.”

“No, I am not buying that. We will get you help. We’ll find a way to fix this.” Roberts began to panic.

“No, you can’t. What you can do, is get me into the driver’s seat. I don’t know how long I have left, but I bet it is long enough, to take these jerks for a ride.” Allen tried to smile, as he took his friend’s hand.

Roberts helped him to the front seat, as Allen sat up in the truck. He started the engine, and turned to his friend. “I’ll be looking out for you. No matter where I end up.”

The tires on the truck flew forward, as Roberts stood watching. He was lost. The worst had happened, and he was still there. He couldn’t remember a time Allen was not with him. Then he heard the sirens coming their way. Reality had caught up with them.

As the SUVs flew past, the four hid behind the building, and looked down the road, as Allen led them away. Roberts looked around, trying to find a way to get moving. Inside the gas station, up on a lift, was a car that had been repaired. He lowered it down, and to his surprise it started.

Backing out of the bay, Roberts stopped the car, just as he heard an explosion. Allen had done what he said he would. He kept the task force busy, until the group could get away. In the end, he had lost too much blood. He lost control of the vehicle, as it crashed into a tree and exploded.

Roberts knew what had happened, and for a second, he looked upwards, as if to say goodbye to his friend. Then he turned to the others. "Come on, we have to get out of here."

"That might not have been him." Stephanie said, with tears in her eyes.

"Maybe not, but my gut says it was. I just know he died a hero."

Nova stood looking at the man who rescued her. She did not know what to say or do. If they had not come to the spaceship in the first place, Allen would still be alive. She would still be in a frozen tube. She wondered if that would not have been better, as she felt a wave of emotions that were foreign to her.

"Guys, we may have avoided task force, but I think we have a bigger problem." Jason sounded scared to death. His voice was quivering, as he tried to talk.

"What do you?….Oh my god…" Stephanie's voice trailed off.

As Jason stood there in front of them, his skin had begun to glow. He looked up at them with a look of terror. "I am so sorry."

To be continued….

Night Of the Walkers

Book Two:

Land Of The Undead

Night Of The Walkers

Included next are the first chapters of G.W. Mullins' Best-Selling title

**Rise of The DarkLighter Book One
Dark Awakening**

From the Author of the Best-Selling
Book Series "From The Dead Of Night"

Rise of the Darklighter

Book One

Dark Awakening

To fight evil, you
have to embrace
the darkness.

G.W. Mullins

Rise Of The Dark-Lighter Book One

Dark Awakening

Is Available in Hardback (978-1-64871-256-2), Paperback (978-1-64871-159-6) and various eBook formats worldwide.

Nuestra Señora de la Santa Muerte, also known as Santa Muerte, is an idol, female deity or folk saint in Mexican and Mexican-American Catholicism. The personification of death, she is believed to be associated with healing, protection, and delivering her devotees safely into the afterlife. Many consider her an angel of death.

Before

The lightning struck around them, as Malachi struggled to steer the car through the debris that the storm threw in their way. His heart raced and he could feel the pounding in his chest. He was scared, probably more scared than he had ever been before. For once in his self-absorbed life, this was not about him, a life was on the line.

"Hang on Uncle, I am doing my best to get us to the hospital. The storm is not making this easy." Malachi tried to comfort him.

"I know, I am holding on. You know I never said how proud I am of you." Carl's voice trailed off into a cough.

"Be still Uncle. There will be time for that after I get you to the hospital."

As Malachi spoke, he attempted to wipe the condensation from the windshield of the car. His efforts were in vain, as he would finish wiping, the fogginess would return. The car was old and barely drivable, it should not have been on the road, but in this situation, he had no choice.

As Malachi looked away to slap his hand against the defroster, he took his eyes off the road. It was then the storm took its vengeance and a funnel cloud passed in front of them. As its winds ripped through the road, a huge oak tree began to sway. Malachi looked up just in time to see it uprooted and flying towards the car.

Malachi let out a scream, as he knew there was nothing he could do to get out of the tree's path. As the tree hit the front grill of the car, it spun out of control and rolled down the deserted street. Flipping end over end, the crushed vehicle landed at the white picket fence that surrounded a country church.

As he looked out through the broken windshield, Malachi felt the blood running down his forehead. Struggling to lift his arm to his head, he felt the pain of being thrown around the vehicle in the crash. He was not sure, but the pain in his chest felt like a cracked rib. The pain came in jabs with his every movement. At first, he did not think of his uncle, then the realization hit him, he was not hearing any noise from the back seat.

Malachi turned to look around. A feeling of dread washed over him. How could his uncle have survived? The man was at death's door before the crash. Looking to the backseat, there was nothing. He was alone in the car.

Looking up through the broken glass, he scanned the road, until he found the form of a body laying several feet behind. His heart sank as he assumed the worst. He had failed with is most important thing he had ever had to do. Pushing against the seat, Malachi attempted to move his battered body to the driver's side door. He pulled the handle and leaned in, but the door was bent and mangled.

Leaning back, Malachi pulled his legs to his chest. He felt the surge of pain as he tried to hold them back with his arms. With all the energy he could muster, he let loose and kicked the door. It flew open quickly, and with such a force, that it slammed into the fender and then to the ground.

Malachi crawled out of the opening and fell to his knees. His head spun around, as dizziness overtook him. The rain blasted all around, as he tried to look towards his uncle. With every drop that hit his head, the blood that covered him splattered and ran down his face. It was no time, before his entire face was covered in red. His eyes stung and burned as he tried to focus, and began to try to get to his feet.

He wobbled back and forth, and lost his footing, falling to the ground as soon as he stood up. He was determined. His mind raced and his life flashed before him. He had accomplished nothing in the twenty years he had been alive. His past was a blur of selfishness and a desire to acquire money.

As he slammed into the paved road, his parent's faces ran through his mind. He wondered if they would have been ashamed of him. He never considered it before. They died when he was very young. He barely knew them. It was then his uncle Carl came and took him in. Malachi felt tears welling in his burning eyes, as he realized the only person on earth that cared for him, was just a few feet away and dying.

Malachi pushed his hands onto the pavement and forced himself upwards. Crawling at first, he finally got his footing and made his way to the lifeless body he saw before him. He fell to his knees at Carl's side and screamed out.

"Be still young one, I am not dead yet." A quiet shaky voice came from Carl's lips.

"Uncle, you are alive. I thought you were…"

"Dead…you can say the word. We all must die sometime, just not this minute. Perhaps soon though." Carl began to cough with his last words.

"No, I will get you help. I promise you I will."

"Malachi, just calm yourself. Go to the church and see if anyone is there. If the priest is in, get him to come and bring me inside."

Malachi rose to his feet, and moved as quickly as he could, to the church doors. As he pulled at the handles, the doors did not move. They were locked. Malachi knew he had to find a way to get his uncle out of the storm. He drew back his fists and threw them at the red wooden door. He screamed out, as he beat on the wood, and threw himself against it trying to force his way in. Just as he was about to give up, the door opened.

"What is happening here?" Father Timothy said hastily as he looked down and saw the bloody face of Malachi. "What has happened to you my boy?"

"The storm, it caused the car to crash and my uncle is badly hurt."

"Why would you come out in a mess like this anyway?" The priest asked.

"My uncle was ill before we left, I think he is dying. Please, can you help him?"

The two made their way to Carl, who was passing in and out of consciousness. Father Timothy took hold of him, and Malachi assisted as they lifted Carl from the ground. The rain pounded down heavily upon them, as they made their way to the door of the church.

Safely inside, they laid Carl's limp body on a pew, near the front of the chapel. Carl's lips moved as if he was speaking to someone. Malachi was not sure of who, he was not sure he wanted to know. He was only sure he was more scared than he had ever been. He looked down at his hands, as they shook uncontrollably. He tried not to succumb to his fears.

The priest returned with towels and a cup of hot tea. As he reached down to Malachi, the boy just looked up to him, barely able to form words. Taking the drink, Malachi held it in his hands, warming them as the priest began to wipe the blood from his forehead and face. Malachi smiled at him trying to find the strength to say thank-you.

"Your uncle needs help that I cannot provide. I can take care of the spiritual end, but honestly, that will not save him. He needs a doctor and medicine. From the looks of him, he was having a heart attack, long before you came out into the storm." Father Timothy said as he continued to clean Malachi's wounds.

"How do we get a doctor? The storm is worse than before. I cannot go anywhere without a car." The boy said, as he hung his head.

"You cannot go anywhere regardless, you are injured. The storm is no place for you in your condition. I will go. I know the roads, and a few shortcuts."

"But how will you get there? You can't walk in this storm."

"I have a motorcycle. It was donated to the church years ago. and I have become very good at riding it. Don't look at me like that, I might be a priest, but I can do normal things you know. Stay here and watch over your uncle. I will be back as soon as I can."

"Father, please be careful. Oh, and thank-you for what you are about to do."

Timothy acknowledged him, and turned to go. Malachi admired his bravery. He wished he was braver than he was. He returned to his uncle's side looking down at him. Carl was still moving his mouth as if he were speaking. The words were not intelligible, but still he spoke under his breath.

As Malachi watched, his uncle's eyes flew open and he pulled his arms close to his chest. Calling out, his voice began to make sense, and his words were clearer. He looked to Malachi and stretched out an arm to grab at him.

Malachi went down on his knees and took his uncle's hand. "What is it uncle. Are you feeling better?"

"No, my boy, I am fighting. The demons of death are coming for me. I need help to fight them. I need you to pray for me. Pray to Santa Muerte, ask her to help me. She will come."

"Uncle, she is not real, she is only a myth. Old Spanish women prey to her as a way to escape their unhappiness." Malachi insisted.

"She is not a myth, she is real. I have known many who have seen her, she comes when life is about to end. She can save me. Please do this for me. You must give her an offering. Place a bowl of water at the alter and pray to her."

"I do not believe in this or in religion, but if it will calm you, I will do it. Now rest as I go find water."

As Malachi searched through the building, he found the kitchen and a bowl for the water. As he filled it, he shook his head, not believing he was about to participate in this craziness. In his heart he knew he had to do it, if for no other reason, to calm his uncle until help came.

Malachi returned to the chapel and placed the water near a statue and cross, in the front of the room. As he kneeled on the floor, he looked up at the Virgin Mary. He wished he believed, in this religion, or in anything that would help them. His heart was too cold and barren he thought.

As he bowed his head, he began to ask for help from Santa Muerte. He asked her to come to him, to aid him in the saving of his uncle. He offered her the bowl of water as an act of respect. Then he closed his eyes. He called for help, and the darkness answered back.

The light in the room faded, as a shadow came forward from the darkened back wall. The figure of a woman took shape. She had dark features and her head was bowed. As she slowly walked forward, Malachi looked up. He prepared to scream, as she raised a shriveled finger to her dried lips.

As he looked at her, he could make out her face, it was drawn and looked as if she had been dead. She retained the features of a woman, but was as much skeleton as human. Her skin looked as if it had been wrapped around bone with no real meat left to her body. Malachi was scared, and his heart raced as she slowly moved towards him.

As she came in his direction, Malachi fell backwards from the feet of the statue. He scrambled trying to get upright. A scream became trapped in his lips as he crawled to the side of his uncle.

Leaning down, Santa Muerte picked up the bowl of water. She moved it to her leathery looking lips and allowed the water to pass into her mouth. She drank until the water was gone. Then she sat the bowl back down and turned towards them.

Malachi stared at her, as she began to smile. As he looked, her appearance began to change. With every second, she became more human in appearance. Her skeletal structure became more flesh-like. Her body filled out, and her face became normal. She laughed out-loud as the transformation became complete.

"Your offering is accepted. I needed that. But why have you disturbed my sleep. It has been many years since I graced this plane. No one has called out to me in over a decade." Santa Muerte looked at him inquisitively.

"My uncle, he is ill. I fear he is dying. Please save him." Malachi pleaded with her.

Extending a hand, she reached down and touched Carl's head. She smiled at him as Carl looked back to her. A joy rushed over him as he saw that Malachi had done as he asked. Carl sat up as Santa Muerte cradled him in her arms.

"Your time to leave this plane was not meant to be as of yet." She spoke softly.

"What do you mean? Is he not dying?"

"That is not what I meant. He was not supposed to die for some time yet. His fate has changed."

"Can you save him?" Malachi pleaded for answers.

"It does not work that way ignorant boy. Life cannot just be given. It is an exchange. A life for a life. One forfeits, so another may live. For him to continue in this existence, another must take his place in death. Now that wouldn't be fair, would it boy?" She asked him.

"No, but I do not want him to die. You have to save him."

"Not everything is by your human choosing. If he is to live, then you tell me whose life to claim in his place. Would you choose that I take the life of the priest that left here unselfishly trying to save another, or perhaps another innocent who does not even know you. Or perhaps, you are willing to exchange your life for his?" She laughed out hysterically, as she walked around looking at the statues in the church.

"No, this cannot be. Malachi, do not even consider her offer. If this is the only way, then I choose death. Take me now Angel of Death. I believed in you and what you stand for. I had no idea you were so cruel and heartless." Carl screamed at her.

"Heartless," she laughed. "I am here to save you, and you call me heartless. I should strike you down myself for your disrespect. I was human like you, and I know the pain of death. You lived much longer than I did. Do not whine to me about your pathetic life. If you want to live, a choice must be made."

"Is there no other way?" Malachi pleaded with her.

"Perhaps, there is. I tire of coming here to this existence to take lives. Become my apprentice, help in my work. Then in the time of one year, you can win back your freedom, if you fulfill your duties."

"You mean, I would not die, and I can come back to my life."

"As pathetic as it is. Yes, you can return, but only at a time I agree. Your Uncle will live, and may do so until his actual time of death that was ordained."

"Then I agree to your terms." Malachi choked on his words.

"No, Malachi do not let her take you. She will not honor the deal. Run from here." Carl screamed.

"It is too late old man, I have him now. The deal is struck. He is mine."

As she turned to look back at Carl, she reached out a hand and Malachi took it. As they walked towards the back hall of the church, they both faded into darkness. Carl stood up, feeling the energy flowing through him again. He was healed, and his life returned. Malachi was not so lucky.

Chapter 1 - Out of The Past

Santa Muerte stood looking, through her portal into the past. She thought about her new apprentice. She watched as he slept. Her mind raced to when she was still human. Moving her hand over the portal, she saw the mist change within, the images went back to the time of 1847. The Mexican-American war raged through Texas. She stared on until she saw herself.

She clung to her mother, as they made their way through the side street trying to avoid the spray of bullets. Her mother pulled her close. Fear covered her face; she had no idea how to save them. They were surrounded by the fighting.

As her mother pulled her into the shelter at the end of the house, Anna looked up to her. She did not understand what was happening. Her mother clung to her trying to quiet her cries.

"Anna…" Her mother spoke. Santa Muerte played the moment over and over again. It had been so long since she had heard her own name said, or her mother's voice saying it. Her cold heart throbbed in her chest. She wasn't supposed to feel this way anymore. She had given up feeling anything about life or people years ago. It was too much of a toll on her. When she inherited her role as an angel of death, she left so much behind.

Looking back into the past, she watched her mother as she cared for Anna who was only six. This war was no place for her. Children were supposed to be carefree and happy. She should have been playing somewhere in a field of flowers. Instead, she was facing an army of soldiers. Santa Muerte glanced down for a moment, she knew what was coming, and that much could still hurt her.

"Mi amor, I promise this is not what I planned for you in life. Please, no matter what happens, remember mama loved you so much. If I could have changed this, I would have. I just do not know how to save you or myself."

As Carlotta finished speaking, she heard the soldiers making their way down the side street. She pulled Anna close and covered her mouth. "Do not cry, do not make a sound." She whispered, as the door began to open slowly. Carlotta raised her head as she came eye to eye with the enemy she had come to fear.

"Stand up woman." He screamed at her.

"Please, I beg of you, spare my child." She cried out.

As the soldier studied her, he did not care for her or her child. He raised his rifle into the air. A smile crossed his lips, as he prepared to claim another notch for his collection of kills. The shot rang out, as Anna watched her mother fall sideways on the ground.

Anna screamed and grabbed at her mother. She pulled at Carlotta's hand, but she did not move.

Anna struggled to arouse her mother, it was no use, she was gone. The young girl had no concept of death or murder. In that day, she witnessed both within minutes. She stood looking at her mother and screaming, as the soldier reloaded his rifle.

"Looks like my lucky day, two Mexicans at the same time. Don't worry, it will be over soon." He said laughing at Anna.

She stood there watching, paralyzed by her own fear. Santa Muerte yelled at her, "Why don't you run and hide. Just save yourself." She raised her hands to her head, as the sound of the rifle firing, rang through the room. Clutching her chest, she caressed the point where the bullet had hit her. If she still had a heart, she thought it would hurt.

Her eyes filled with tears as she watched. The soldier left, walking away proud of himself and his deeds. She felt hatred filling her. She grinned, and thought to herself, there must still be some emotions left inside somewhere. As the killer turned to leave the alley, a Mexican soldier came from around the corner and fired before he was seen. The murderer fell to the ground, a grim look on his face. As he looked up, he saw the dark one coming for him.

A few feet away, the dark shadow came. As it moved forward, it took shape. A man emerged from within the darkness. Dressed in black from head to toe, he wore a dress suit and looked like an undertaker. Looking about, the dark one studied the area. "So many dead, so many souls to claim. I'll be here a while." The Angel of Death was pleased.

He cleared the street of the dead before surveying the area. He made his way down the street until finding the bodies of Carlotta and Anna. Looking down at Anna, he shook his head. "Little One, you never had a chance in life, did you?"

As he lifted Anna into his arms, he carried her through the streets. His pain was obvious, as he struck out at those who caused the death of such a young girl. In moments, he killed all who were in the immediate area, before lifting himself upwards with the child still in his arms.

In his own realm, he took Anna to his private chamber. There he took a small amount of his power and formed a ball of energy in front of him. Looking down at the girl, he aimed his hand, shooting the power within her. "My child, forgive me for what I do, but this is the only way I know to give you life again." With the power surging through her, she took a deep breath, and sat up coughing.

"Arise Muerte. My child, born of death."

"My name is Anna, she said staring at him."

"You were Anna, now you are so much more. You are Queen of the Dead."

"I don't understand." She questioned him.

"In time, it will all make sense to you. But for now, you will grow and learn."

As his words echoed through the room, Malachi watched from behind. He had been watching the whole time. He understood a little better what was happening. He had enlisted his soul with that of the dead.

Chapter 2 – The Dead Are Still Among Us

Malachi looked on in disbelief, as the history of Muerte unfolded. Pulling back in fear, he knew his fate was far worse than he ever imagined. In his thoughts, he realized he had signed on to be a servant of death. Sitting back on the bed, he pulled his knees to his chest, as fear overtook him.

Muerte watched, until her history was more than she could take. A tear dropped from her eye, landing on her hand. She looked down in amazement, at the idea she could produce such a foreign object. Moisture was a fleeting idea to her. Without it, she was a mere wraith. Raising her hand to eye level, she admired the wetness of her hand. She moved her hand back and forth, allowing the tear to move slowly at her will. Smiling at it, as she manipulated it. Then, she gently pulled her hand to her mouth and savored the salty wetness. The mere sensation thrilled her for a moment, but it was fleeting. There was little room in her life for joy.

Her body needed all the moisture she could claim. Without the offerings of her followers, she would revert to her dry skeletal form. Her many years in the land of the dead, had turned her once beautiful skin to dried leather stretched over bone. Her last years of seeking solitude and rest, had not boded well to her physical form.

With a wave of her hand, Muerte cleared the view portal. She sighed as she turned away, to see Malachi sitting behind, his fear showing like a beacon. She knew instantly he had seen her. As her eyes met his, she gave him a sinister grin. Her head bowed in a way that she looked up at him in a glare.

"You were human once." He spoke trembling.

"Little boys, who do not mind their business, like a curious cat, can end up dead. You have been warned, for now I will allow the intrusion. We all have to start somewhere, but it is the journey that defines us." Muerte laughed in a ghoulishly morbid way.

"Are you really going to let me go if I serve you?" He said standing up, and moving back from her.

"I will honor my word. As long as you do as I ask. Be warned, your freedom will come at a cost. You saw the images; Anna was a sweet innocent child. A short time in the company of Death changed her…to me. In a year of your life here, do you really think you will ever be the same?" She said turning to leave.

"What will you ask of me? What am I expected to do?" Malachi asked timidly.

"You will go forth and prepare the dead in different times and places. I will choose the place and you will ready people for me to claim."

"What do you mean times?"

"The living, believe in such linear lives. Not everything goes forward in the line of time. In truth, time is irrelevant. Living outside of time, we can move backwards and forwards at will. The dead have to be claimed. If they were not, then hell on earth would be a real thing."

"Are you a servant of God?" Malachi blurted out.

"Oh, you silly boy, the ideas of Heaven and Hell, are so humanized. The rules you were taught in church don't apply here. There is an upper realm and a below for the demons. But here, religion is much more vicious. It is a competition to claim the dead, for the side of good or evil." She turned and studied him closely.

"Why do you look at me like that?" He asked nervously.

"The effects of this realm have already begun to affect you. Your veins are darkening, one would have thought you were a demon before you came here. Maybe it is your selfishness coming forward. You should have believed in something in life." She laughed, "Or maybe not, it did not help me much."

"When I am freed, will this go away? Will I look human again?" he asked running his fingers over his arm.

"One can only hope." She walked away leaving Malachi to look at his skin. He raised his arm slowly and studied the dark veins that ran through his body. He was transforming into something of which he had no idea.

Muerte walked the hall, passing one empty room after another. As she floated past, she glanced into them. Inside as she watched, a scene came to life. There, wars played out, as did natural disasters. In some, there were images of the dead collecting together as spirits. Malachi ran behind her and watched the rooms. As he followed, his vision changed, his eyes darkened to a point the images of death were clear to him. He could see what she did, and that frightened him.

Muerte turned to him and looked him in the eyes. "Your transformation has given you the gift of after-sight. Your eyes have turned dark. Now you will see what the dead see. If someone is dying, you will be able to see the change and the approach of death. If they are already dead, you will be able to see what is left of their spirit. You will see all existence, from all realms. It is a gift, and at the same time a curse you have been given. One day you will learn to hate what has been thrust upon you. In this year, do not let it rob the humanity you have left."

"I can see into the rooms. What do they mean?"

"They are times, in the future and the past. You will be sent to them to claim those dead or about to die. And sometimes, you will have to help things along." She lowered her head.

"Wait, you mean I will have to kill. I never agreed to that. I don't know if I am capable." He yelled.

"Oh, shut your mouth. Do I look as if I have time for whining? If you want your freedom, you will do as you are told. Now, look into this room.

Do you see this cemetery? It will be your first travel. You will go there, and claim the dead who occupy the cemetery. Be warned, there is one there who is powerful enough to stop you in your goals. Do not underestimate him, or what he is capable of. There is a rumor that a war is coming. He will be the deciding factor of whether good or evil rules." Muerte pointed to the room, and the blond boy who traveled the cemetery.

"What if he tries to stop me?" Malachi asked.

"Don't let him." She said evilly.

"What happens if the boy loses his battle for good and evil?" Malachi asked looking intently at the blond boy.

"The dead will claim the earth. No spirits will cross into the light. I will not be able to collect the dead. In short, the dead will inhabit the earth and the living will go into chaos. It will be Armageddon, a gathering of armies for a battle in the end of times."

"Who would win such a battle?" Malachi nervously whispered.

"No one. I imagine the dead being more powerful, would win the war. They want so badly to find a way to go back to being human. When they do not pass over, they just roam forever, ignored by the ones they loved in life. They become jealous, maybe even envious of the living, who can still interact and have a life. They end up in a place of despair and hurt. Then they are susceptible to the preying of a higher-level demon. If that happens, they are finished. The demon will drain them of power, and use it to become more powerful themselves. The spirit then fades to nothing, kind of like a drug addict. They just simply fade away until they are gone."

"And when there are only the demons?" He asked

"They kill each other until there is one. Life as you knew it, would cease to exist." She bowed her head, as she walked into and open room with no images. Nothing existed there but emptiness and a dark foreboding gloom.

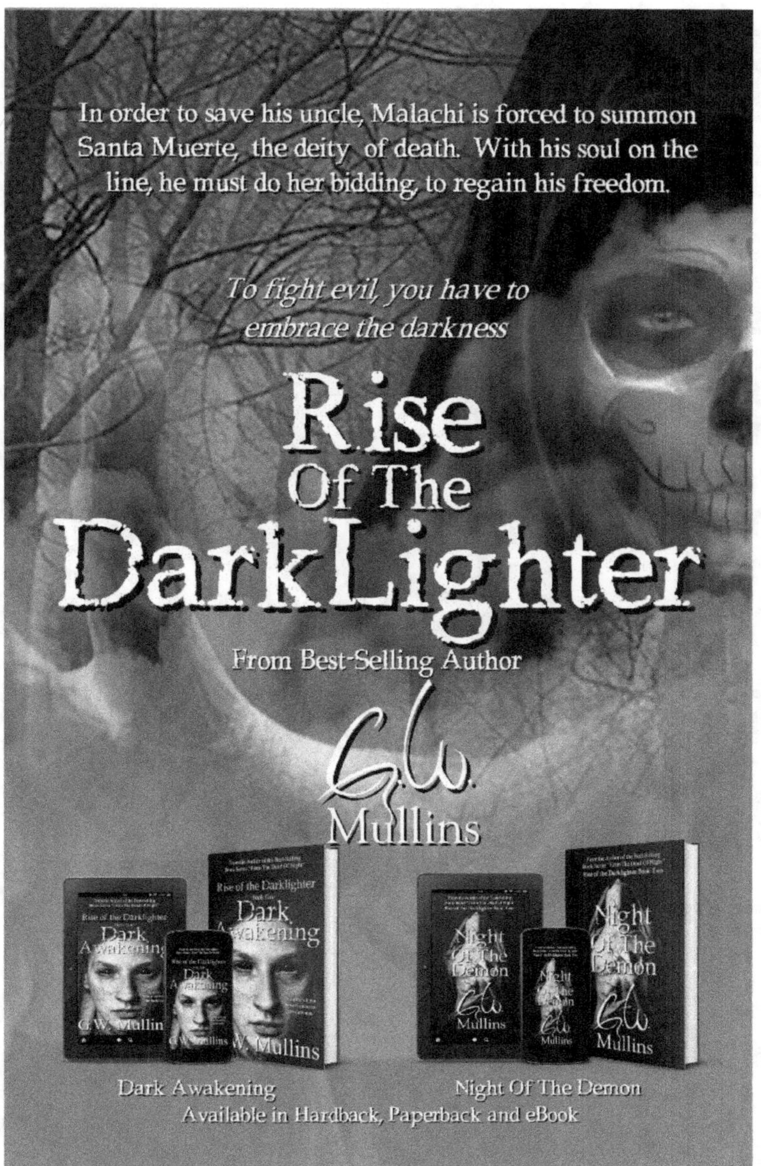
In order to save his uncle, Malachi is forced to summon
Santa Muerte, the deity of death. With his soul on the
line, he must do her bidding, to regain his freedom.

To fight evil, you have to
embrace the darkness

Rise
Of The
DarkLighter

From Best-Selling Author

G.W.
Mullins

Dark Awakening   Night Of The Demon
Available in Hardback, Paperback and eBook

Mullins

About the Author

Thanks for choosing this book, if you enjoyed it, please leave positive feedback.

G.W. Mullins is an Author, Photographer, and Entrepreneur of Native American / Cherokee descent. He has been a published author for over 13 years. His writing has focused on the paranormal and Native American studies.

Mullins has released several books on the history/stories/fables of the Native American Indians. Among his books are the extremely successful "Star People, Sky Gods and Other Tales of the Native American Indians," "Story Teller An Anthology Of Folklore From The Native American Indians," "The Native American Story Book - Stories Of The American Indians For Children Volumes 1-5," "The Native American Cookbook," and "Walking With Spirits Native American Myths, Legends, And Folklore Volumes 1 Thru 6."

He has released the complete series of his Sci/fi Fantasy books "From The Dead Of Night," including the Best-Selling titles – "Daniel Is Waiting" and

"Daniel Returns." His most recent work includes the series "Rise Of The Snow Queen" featuring Book One "The Polar Bear King", Book Two "War Of The Witches", and Book Three "The Story of Gerda And Kai."

Mullins' latest releases include two young adult fantasy series, "Rise of the Darklighter" Book One "Dark Awakening," Book Two "Night Of The Demon" and the "Dream Walker" Book Series featuring "Enter the Sandman" and "Wide Awake In Dream Land." Among his other releases are "The Legend Of White Bear (Extended edition)" a Native American paranormal shapeshifting story, "Messages from The Other Side" (a nonfiction book about communication with the dead), and the currently releasing "The Convergence" (a post-apocalyptic book multi-series event).

For further information, on his writing, visit G.W. Mullins' web site at ***http://gwmullins.wix.com/books***.

Daniel walked
in the land of
the dead.
Now the dead
want him
back!

For Information About

From The Dead
Of Night
The Book Series Visit
gwmullins.wixsite.com/books

<u>Also Available From G.W. Mullins</u>

The Convergence Book Zero Mass Destruction

The Convergence Book One Armageddon

Rise of the Darklighter Book One Dark Awakening

Rise of the Darklighter Book Two Night Of The Demon

Rise Of The Snow Queen Book Three The Story Of Gerda And Kai

Rise Of The Snow Queen Book Two The War Of The Witches

Rise Of The Snow Queen Book One The Polar Bear King

Daniel Awakens A Ghost Story Begins– From The Dead Of Night Prequel

Daniel Is Waiting A Ghost Story – From The Dead Of Night Book One

Night Of The Walkers

Daniel Returns A Ghost Story - From The Dead Of
Night Book Two

Daniel's Fate A Ghost Story Ends - From The Dead
Of Night Book Four

Dream Walker Book Two Wide Awake In Dream
Land

Dream Walker Book One Enter The Sand Man

Nick Grainger Book One The Curse Of Cleopatra

The Legend Of White Bear (Extended Edition)

Messages From The Other Side Stories of the Dead,
Their Communication, and Unfinished Business

Vengeance – A Paranormal Mystery

Mysteries Of The Unseen World – Ghost, Hauntings
and The Unexplained

Haunted America Stories Of Ghost, Hauntings And
The Unexplained

Timeless – A Paranormal Romance Murder Mystery

Mullins

Star People, Sky Gods, And Other Tales Of The
Native American Indians

More Star People, Sky Gods, And Other Paranormal
Tales Of The Native American Indians

Aliens, Gods, and other Paranormal Native American
Tales

Buffalo Tales Of The Native American Indians

Coyote Tales Of The Native American Indians

Bear Tales Of The Native American Indians

Lost Tales Of The Native American Indians Vol 1

Lost Tales Of The Native American Indians Vol 2

Walking With Spirits Native American Myths,
Legends, And Folklore Volumes One Thru Six

The Native American Cookbook

Native American Cooking - An Indian Cookbook
With Legends And Folklore

Night Of The Walkers

The Native American Story Book - Stories Of The
American Indians For Children
Volumes One Thru Five

The Best Native American Stories For Children

Cherokee A Collection of American Indian Legends,
Stories And Fables

Creation Myths - Tales Of The Native American
Indians
Strange Tales Of The Native American Indians

Spirit Quest - Stories Of The Native American
Indians

Animal Tales Of The Native American Indians

Medicine Man - Shamanism, Natural Healing,
Remedies And Stories Of The Native American
Indians

Native American Legends: Stories Of The Hopi
Indians Volumes One and Two

Totem Animals Of The Native Americans

The Best Native American Myths, Legends And
Folklore Volumes One Thru Three

Ghosts, Spirits And The Afterlife In Native American
Indian Mythology And Folklore

War Song: Tales Of The Native American Indians

Origin Tales Of The Native American

Night Of The Walkers

For books available from G.W. Mullins in Hardback,
Paperback and eBook

Visit: https://gwmullins.wixsite.com/books

Or scan the QR Code below

Links to G.W. Mullins pages are on Linktree
https://linktr.ee/gw.mullins